THE HUNT FOR THE TREASURE SHIP!

Plainly, the second mate bore important news. Long Rube came over the side like a monkey and beckoned Forrester to the rail. The two mates stood in low-voiced conversation for a brief moment, then Bower tumbled down into his boat again and pulled for shore.

To the surprise of Blake, Forrester sent a hail forward for him.

"How much fo'c's'le talk have you heard, Dude?" asked the big mate, when the two stood together at the rail. "You got some idee what we're after?"

"Some," admitted Blake, eyeing the man keenly. "Not much."

"All right. Howard's the skipper o' the *John Foster*, yonder. He's got a girl aboard. The girl is after the wreck of a ship sunk some'eres between here and Australia. Steelfist is after it too, see? But we don't know where the wreck lays, an' prob'ly the crew o' the *Foster* does — they'll know where they're bound for, anyhow."

Blake nodded quietly.

"The Ol' Man is goin' to come aboard later. Crew's goin' ashore. You an' me go ashore tonight, see? We got a scheme on what'll work. But you talk turkey right now, Dude. Do you stick with us or not? You're no liar, an' I owe you a good turn anyhow; say yes or no, and either way goes as she lays with me."

"I say yes," returned Blake, his gray eyes steady.

"Good for you, bully! Then don't go ashore with the boys, that's all."

MORE WILDSIDE CLASSICS

Dacobra, or The White Priests of Ahriman, by Harris Burland
The Nabob, by Alphonse Daudet
Out of the Wreck, by Captain A. E. Dingle
The Elm-Tree on the Mall, by Anatole France
The Lance of Kanana, by Harry W. French
Amazon Nights, by Arthur O. Friel
Caught in the Net, by Emile Gaboriau
The Gentle Grafter, by O. Henry
Raffles, by E. W. Hornung
Gates of Empire, by Robert E. Howard
Tom Brown's School Days, by Thomas Hughes
The Opium Ship, by H. Bedford Jones
The Miracles of Antichrist, by Selma Lagerlof
Arsène Lupin, by Maurice LeBlanc
A Phantom Lover, by Vernon Lee
The Iron Heel, by Jack London
The Witness for the Defence, by A.E.W. Mason
The Spider Strain and Other Tales, by Johnston McCulley
Tales of Thubway Tham, by Johnston McCulley
The Prince of Graustark, by George McCutcheon
Bull-Dog Drummond, by Cyril McNeile
The Moon Pool, by A. Merritt
The Red House Mystery, by A. A. Milne
Blix, by Frank Norris
Wings over Tomorrow, by Philip Francis Nowlan
The Devil's Paw, by E. Phillips Oppenheim
Satan's Daughter and Other Tales, by E. Hoffmann Price
The Insidious Dr. Fu Manchu, by Sax Rohmer
Mauprat, by George Sand
The Slayer and Other Tales, by H. de Vere Stacpoole
Penrod (Gordon Grant Illustrated Edition), by Booth Tarkington
The Gilded Age, by Mark Twain
The Blockade Runners, by Jules Verne
The Gadfly, by E.L. Voynich

Please see www.wildsidepress.com for a complete list!

SHIPS OF STRIFE
CAPTAIN A. E. DINGLE

WILDSIDE PRESS

SHIPS OF STRIFE

"Ships of Strife" originally appeared in *The Argosy*, June 1916.

This edition published in 2006 by Wildside Press, LLC.
www.wildsidepress.com

CHAPTER I

NOT THE SCRAP HE EXPECTED

Standing on the club steps, Jack Blake directed his chauffeur to take the car home without him. Then he turned to the noisy and vociferous group of men filling the doorway at his back. At sound of his voice they fell silent.

"A bet of five hundred is worth a scrap, boys," he smiled. "But I won't have any. I'll show up to claim those stakes, all intact, and with three cool drinks of milk inside me!"

"Yes, you will!" echoed the derisive shout, halting Blake as he started down the steps to the sidewalk. "You'll come back with that topper smashed and your coat-tails torn off, old sport! Bet you another hundred you call in the cops!"

"You're on!" exclaimed Blake sharply. "So long!"

Tucking his stick beneath his arm, he gave his silk hat a natty tip with a Cohanesque pat of the hand; then he vanished into the fog which had drifted in from the Golden Gate to hide the stars and to cloak all San Francisco in darkness.

The Millionaires' Club was the home of freak bets, but Jack Blake had that night provided the liveliest game of all. A heated discussion had ended in the wager that Blake, correctly attired in evening dress, could not procure three drinks of milk in as many waterfront saloons — and return intact to tell the tale.

Blake himself had some doubt over his ability to win that wager, but his confidence in Jack Blake banished his forebodings. Nor was this self-confidence founded on egotism and the possession of worldly pelf, as a glance at his face alone would have shown.

This, the youngest member of the Millionaires' Club, was indubitably a good-looking man. He had never had to work for his living, and had devoted his energy to having a good time — in his own way.

His keen gray eyes held the promise of powerful character, should that character ever be evoked into action; so, too, did thin nostrils, the thin, curved lips and the out-jutting bone of the chin which Blake had inherited from his fighting father.

As a polo-player, Blake was known from Coronado to Newport; as an amateur boxer he was of far less renown, though of accomplished skill, for his blazing temper was little suited to the ring.

Being his own master and having plenty of this world's goods, Jack Blake had no quarrel with life. Twenty-three, a passable athlete and something of a boxer, he considered himself the equal of any man alive. And, being convinced that the waterfront was not so bad as it was painted, he broke into a cheerful whistle as he strode along.

Fresh from a perfect dinner — for the club chef was an admitted master of his art — Jack Blake bubbled over with the wine of youth and good spirits. As he sniffed hard at the swirling gray fog, laden with the brine of the Pacific, his pulse leaped high in keen anticipation of his adventure.

He cut short the cheerful whistle, but only for the instant required to relieve himself of a ringing laugh of pure exhilaration. Then the whistle pealed out afresh, echoing eerily back to him from the murky caverns of gray that enveloped all things.

It was yet early for the denizens of the waterfront. Of course, the dives would shelter their habitués at every hour of the day — Blake had a vivid recollection of a previous slumming excursion to the "North Pole," where he had witnessed a real bottle fight in broad daylight.

Yet, to give his club-fellows a sporting run for their money, he determined to take his initial drink of milk at a time when life down there was in full blast.

With this praiseworthy resolve, Blake spent half an hour in "dead reckoning" navigation of the blanketed streets by means of the greater lights of the street corners. The ordinary lamps along the sidewalks only became visible when he bumped into their standards.

As a thicker blanket of gray drifted up the sloping streets from the sea, Blake, with a shiver, buttoned the light overcoat which partially concealed his evening attire. The fog grew colder as he struck into Montgomery Avenue and headed down toward the ferry slips.

He had now had sufficient of this aimless wandering. It was high time, he thought, to set to work to win that wager.

Although more accustomed to be carried in his car than to walk, he had some acquaintance with the streets hereabouts and was quite conversant with his general direction. When, in a brief instant of clarity, he found himself at the corner where Montgomery Street joined the avenue, he turned to the left and headed for the Custom House.

Now in front, Blake could catch fleeting glimpses of glaring lights at the ferry-slips. For what seemed limitless leagues of darkness, the outer night shrieked and boomed with the whistles of watercraft.

Blake picked out the sparsely lighted windows of the Custom House and the brighter illumination of the post office close by. Right across the street was the dark waterfront. There lay his cruising ground, or at least his entrance to it.

As he neared the post office, a forlorn-looking hack drew up to the curb, discharged two fares, and lumbered off into the fog. The two passengers were brought into prominence by a lifting of the mist.

Blake saw that one was a quietly dressed girl, the other a burly, bow-legged, powerful-looking man.

These two stood in conversation for an instant, then the man disappeared into the dim doorway of the Custom House. The girl stepped into the blaze of light in the post office door and vanished likewise.

Blake found himself staring in most unmannerly fashion as the light shone upon the girl's slender figure, and he pulled himself up with a sharp inward rebuke. In that single instant of observation he had noted two interesting facts.

First, the girl was pretty, refined and even piquant — despite the curl-destroying dampness that fringed her small hat with glistening rime. Second, she wore an air of serious business which sat strangely upon her shapely shoulders; the swing of her walk bespoke poise, self-confidence and a fixity of purpose which interested Blake.

An instant later he collided squarely with interesting fact number three.

He squared off on his course for the waterfront, crossed the shaft of light thrown by the post office doorway, and ran into a man who stepped out of the darkness.

The man's face was turned toward the doorway. His eyes glared after the girl's figure with a wolfish glitter that blazed into wrath as Jack Blake bumped into him.

"Where in Hades you coming?" he snarled. "You keep your eyes in the boat, Willie, an' beat it!"

Blake sent a keen look over the man, with a host of possibilities crowding into his mind.

The fellow was a good two inches taller than Blake, who brushed the bar at five feet eleven. His glittering eyes glowed like black diamonds in deep cavities under bushy brows; the shoulders of a Hercules terminated in huge, black-gloved hands at the end of gorilla-like arms; crisp black curls framed a savage face that was tanned to a brick hue and heavily lined and seamed.

Blake apologized civilly enough to this scowling personage, but not through fear. He then walked on to the Custom House and stood, hidden by the curtain of fog, watching the streak of light at the post office doorway.

"I wonder," he mused reflectively, "what connection there is between that girl and her first escort, and this powerful savage who seems so interested? She's pretty far removed from their stratum, or I'm no judge! I guess I'll forget milk for a bit."

From this vantage point Blake could see the figure of the "savage" lurking just outside the edge of light. At frequent intervals the scowling face protruded from the rim of fog and peered into the doorway; to Blake it looked ludicrously like the head of a midway gentleman who invites the attention of "three balls for a nickel."

At this hour the streets were practically deserted. Those who might have had business in the district were glad to accept the fog as an excuse to postpone it. Only when a ferryboat pulled into the slip did a few scurrying figures pass up or down the street.

Blake, feeling the chill of the mist piercing through his light overcoat, grew impatient as the moments wore along. He had almost decided to abandon his watch when suddenly the girl appeared.

She stepped out to the sidewalk, turned sharply to the right, and walked swiftly past Blake's hiding-place.

Before she was quite swallowed up in the fog the big fellow came striding past, head forward and arms swinging, muttering to himself as he went.

"H'm! Grows interesting!" thought Blake with a thrill of expectancy.

Gripping his stick, he followed. The man, while a scant five yards ahead, had already been lost in obscurity; but the dull, damp pad of rubber heels formed an index to his position. At the corner the footsteps ceased, and Blake halted abruptly.

For the moment he was at a loss.

Then, from the side street near by, he heard voices — a deep rumble, followed by a girl's clear tone that was evidently charged with apprehension. That note of fear dissipated Blake's doubts. He softly stepped nearer until he could make out a dark blur in the fog, then he slipped into the gloom of a side door to the Custom House and waited.

He had to be sure about this, he reflected.

But with the first words, he crammed his silk hat down on his head, took off his gloves, and gripped his light stick tensely.

"Let me pass, sir!" came the girl's voice, "I don't know you."

"You'll know me soon enough, miss," growled the deep tones. "I want to talk a little business with you."

"I don't want to know you!" exclaimed the girl. "And I have no business that could possibly concern you —"

The man's growl broke in and drew a sharp cry from the girl.

"What — impossible! Even if you had credentials, and your ship is what you say, the matter is closed. My arrangements are made. Let me pass, sir!"

"Not me, my beauty! You'll unmake your arrangements tomorrow, understand?"

The girl answered calmly, yet with desperation underlying the calm.

"Get out of my way, or I shall call for help!"

Blake, edging nearer, poised on his toes. He saw the two figures sway together, and then —

"He-e-l-p!"

The girl's quick cry was strangled in its utterance as the big ruffian swung her to him, his hand over her mouth.

Blake waited no longer. In two strides he reached his man. With keen regard for the small possibilities in his stick as a club, he put his weight behind it and gave the point. The man's left arm was half raised; fair in the armpit, swift as a rapier thrust, the steel-tipped cane hit home.

With a smothered curse the girl's assailant dropped his hold upon her, swung around, snatched furiously at the cane and snapped it in two. Then, with a second curse, he plunged headlong at Blake, his huge hands outstretched to grapple.

Jack Blake knew better than this, however. He sidestepped, whipped over a streaking right cross, and the man went down with a crash.

The girl stood bewildered, unable to appreciate what had taken place. Blake swung her rapidly into the doorway he had just left.

"Go inside and leave by the front door," he cried sharply. Then he turned to meet a savage rush that all but hurled him after her.

What happened next occupied, perhaps, something less than two minutes. But those two minutes were crowded with more action than Jack Blake had ever experienced in any six-round amateur contest at the club.

Warily avoiding the clinch his huge opponent desired, Blake used every trick of footwork in his possession, slipping in and out with stinging straight punches. He had need of all he knew.

The grim shape of his enemy bored in with insistence, apparently caring nothing for the shrewdest blows. Then a left swing rocked Blake's head until he heard the bells ringing; there followed a right that made the left swing seem like a feather pillow.

Never in all his bouts had Blake ever received a punch like that one. He spat out a broken tooth, clenched his jaw, and resolved to avoid that right in future.

But in the thickening gloom it was impossible to discern the blows. Blake could hear the savage, short breaths of his opponent; he tried to time his punches, hitting straight out at the breaths. Then he guarded a sweeping right, and his arm felt paralyzed from wrist to elbow.

"Great Scott!" he thought. "That right feels like a club! But he hasn't got knuckles, that's sure —"

He was smothered with a volley of stupefying wallops which swept aside his guard, and again that terrible, uncanny, inhuman right swung into him, fair and square over the heart.

Blake felt himself slipping. His brain fought to retain its balance, and he instinctively fought back, knew that he was hitting hard and solidly; yet the dim figure in front seemed to assume alarming proportions. Once more that awful right drove in over his heart.

Other shapes began to grow out of the fog, but Blake still fought doggedly, clenching back the cry that came to his lips.

He felt the Custom House walls at his back, knew he was giving ground — and could give no more. His chest was bursting. The stranger's right came over his guard and rocked his head back against the brick wall with a thud.

Through Blake's muddled brain came the drum of hurrying feet. His knees gave way and he slipped helplessly to the ground.

As through a red haze he saw that terrible right arm curved back to swing down at him — then a crowd surged around. He heard short, snappy commands, felt himself lifted, and with a dumb prayer of thanks that the police had come, passed into unconsciousness.

But — the police had not come.

CHAPTER II

FOES AND FRIENDS

> *"For grog is our larboard and starboard.*
> *Our mainmast, our mizzen, our log,*
> *On shore, or at sea, or when harbored,*
> *The mariner's compass is grog!"*

Somewhere over his splitting head, Jack Blake heard a cracked, tinpan, maudlin voice blaring out these words. At the end of them came the gluck-gluck of liquid pouring from a bottle neck.

"Huh — did I win that bet?" he thought vaguely. "Wow — this is a head! What happened? Oh, of course — that girl — the scrap —"

He lay quiet, repressing the inward groan that was urged from him. While he quite remembered the scene outside the Custom House, he now seemed to be in a very strange place indeed — so strange that he doubted his own senses.

His extremely misty vision gave him a queer picture of a board shelf just above his head. The bed that his fingers touched, as he half unconsciously groped out, felt strangely unlike the soft, springy couch in his room at the club.

A dull glimmer of wavering, streaky light gave him clear sight of nothing except that board shelf above him. But his head buzzed and ached, while his arms were swollen and raw to the touch. He remembered that terrible right.

"I must have struck a gorilla or a stone man," he thought, trying to bring order out of the chaos in his mind.

He dully closed his eyes to rest the aching nerves. He hoped that his man would have his coffee ready soon. This was —

> *"For grog is our larboard and starboard,*
> *Our mainmast, our — "*

"Shut yer gob, ye guzzlin' swine!"

The new voice was accompanied by something which Blake later learned to know as a serving-mallet. The mallet whizzed out of the darkness and landed with a crunching smack against the head of the singer.

"Blast yer soul!" swore the victim furiously.

His bottle flew through the air, smashing to a thousand slivers of glass, and filling the room with the odor of cheap whisky. The rank smell combined with other smells and formed an inharmonious whole.

Blake started up with a shock of realization. His head bumped the shelf above, and he fell back thoroughly awakened. He put out a leg and felt for the floor — then halted abruptly and stared.

A shape rose up before him; a huge foot trod on his hand; with lurid oaths and a tremendous scuffling, the guzzling singer was hauled down from above Blake, to fall with a crash and crouch on the floor. The larger shape towered above him.

"Hey! Let up, Cutlip! Let up, yuh big stiff!"

The cracked voice broke into whimpering as a heavy boot smashed through weakly guarding arms and landed forcibly on head and ribs, time and again.

"T'row bottles at me, will ye? There, ye hog!"

Cutlip seized the edge of the bunk above Blake in both hands; then he brought both feet savagely down upon the bottle-heaver, who groaned once and relapsed into limp insensibility.

His conqueror stepped to the middle of the floor, flapped his arms in grotesquely drunken imitation of wings, and crowed.

"Urrk-uh-uh-uh-urrk! I'm Cutlip Sullivan, an' I chew 'em up raw! I eat alligator bait an' sharkskin fer dinner! I'm the cock o' the fo'c's'le, by cripes — any other son of a pig want to present me wid a bottle?"

Feeling that this query was hardly addressed to him, Jack Blake swung his legs to the floor, slowly and painfully.

"Will you tell me where I am and how I got there?" he inquired thickly.

Even to himself his voice sounded strange. His throat and lips were swollen and dry. As he tried to stand up he tottered — the floor felt detached from everything and he sat down again heavily.

Cutlip Sullivan stood staring, his mouth half open as if for another crow, and his arms half raised. As he took in the details of Blake's attire, a grin of delight creased his scarred and unholy visage. He stepped closer for a better view.

"By cripes! Look what's wid us! Ain't he the purty critter!"

Jack looked down at himself with a faint grin. His evening dress was torn and mud-spattered, and his broad shirt-bosom befouled with blood. He tenderly felt his features and realized that they must be one mottled, all-embracing bruise.

But wonder grew in him as he stared around. He was in a reeking, half dark, wholly filthy cavern of unpainted wood, triangular in shape. Two double rows of littered bunks ran along the two longer sides to the apex. Against the shorter side stood a noisome tin oil lamp which made little light, but much smell.

A floor upon which a self-respecting pig would develop insomnia; and a grinding, smashing din of heavy chain swinging from side to side in huge, rusted iron pipes — these completed Blake's mental picture. And over against him stood Cutlip Sullivan — a mighty ruffian with a split lip that sneered perpetually at the world.

"Sure, I kin tell where ye are," grinned Cutlip, in drunken and ghastly mirth. "'Tis the good ship *C. H. Marshall* ye're aboard of.

Steelfist Charley Marshall's her skipper, an' she's a hellship from Hades!"

Blake stared at his informant, incredulous. Shanghaied? Impossible!

"But how did I come here? Isn't this ship sailing?"

Sullivan roared with amusement.

"Sure she's sailing me lad! How ye come here I dunno. Mebbe ye paid yer passage, huh? Don't ye like yer cabin 'commodations?"

Shanghaied — in this day of law and order? He, Jack Blake — shanghaied? Then, by the Lord Harry, someone was going to suffer for it!

A storm of rage surged through Blake.

He rose and started toward the only outlet in sight — a rough wooden ladder nailed against the after side of the den, which led through a small, square trap up overhead.

"Better stop where ye are, me lad," advised Cutlip with a drunken leer. "The mate's left us here to git over our jags, mebbe. Bully Forrester ain't the bucko to leave seamen in their bunks if there's any chanct o' using 'em on deck! Wait till yer hauled out, me lad — that'll be quick enough, Heaven knows!"

With which Sullivan raised his own bottle and gurgled.

Overhead, Blake could faintly hear a babel of sounds that spoke eloquently of hard work being done, and of harder driving helping the work. A gray patch of breaking day showed against the square glass in the hatch, crisscrossed by a maze of ropes.

A lifting, roaring shape surged and strained into Blake's sight, then vanished, as the flowing sheeted fore-course snored with wet wind.

Over all rose a strident, powerful voice bawling sturdy sea-oaths in accompaniment to resounding thuds of blows. The voice came nearer, and Cutlip's prophecy was borne out.

A huge bulk filled the hatch. Two thick, sea-booted legs felt for the ladder; and rough and blusterous as a deck-sweeping sea itself, Bully Forrester dropped to the fo'c's'le floor.

He stood stooping, bowed arms hanging to his knees, peering into the dim dark hole.

"Yes, sir, I'm goin'," cried Sullivan, making up the ladder nimbly enough before the mate could speak.

Forrester grinned.

"Up, you sojers! Want any help?" Lurching over toward Blake, Bully Forrester stumbled over the prostrate form of the man on the floor.

"What in — who's this cherub?"

A closer scrutiny satisfied the mate that the Bottle Heaver was far from being an able seaman just at present. Accordingly he put his foot to the man's ribs and shoved him beneath the lower bunk.

Standing erect, he looked at Blake.

"Out o' this, you skulker!" A great fist, knotted as an oak root, was drawn back. Then it dropped slowly, the fingers opening and clutching Jack's arm as Forrester leaned forward to look closer.

"Oh, scissors! You're the dude that put the shiner on the skipper, ain't you? Mister, he'll be plumb tickled to see you!"

Blake savagely shook off the clutching hand. A red gale of anger sweeping him, he stepped to the ladder.

"You bet he will!" he made answer grimly. "And if he thinks he can get away —"

"Hold on there!" growled the mate, seizing Blake's flying coat tails in a firm and determined grip. "Git this in your bean — I'm mate o' this ship! Fo'c's'le dogs say 'sir' to me. Savvy that?"

Blake was too angry for coherent thought. He replied with a wicked uppercut landing with the full swing of his body.

It caught the mate flush on the chin and hurled him against the bunks with a crash. Then Blake leaped for the deck, reached it after a scramble, and looked around.

Dazed by the sudden change from the fetid air of that fo'c's'le to the fresh, crisp gale that poured upon him from beneath the foot of the foresail, Jack Blake staggered unsteadily to the maze of ropes around the foremast. He clung to them, fully satisfied to recuperate for a moment before seeking the skipper.

Looking over the side and weighing his chances of quitting the ship, he saw the coast stretching in a blue line to port, under a heavy gray pall of morning clouds. To starboard, farther distant, the Farralones spiked out of the slate-colored sea, to spike into the slate-colored sky and vanish.

All around him the outlook was gray and dismal. A dreary drizzle of rain fell incessantly, soaking him to the skin. Gray decks, aglisten with dampness, gray sails booming in the wind overhead; sullen, slouching, gray-faced men toiling in the rainy mist coiling up gray ropes. Ugh!

Blake felt the unsteadiness slowly going out of his legs. Under the stinging fresh breeze his blood began to course again.

Despite the damp dreariness of it all, he felt that he was now man enough to interview the skipper of this horrible "hellship," as Cutlip had termed her. He knew dimly that sailors so termed the ship where men were worked hard.

Letting go the foretopsail sheet tackles, to which he had clung, Blake took a few steps to try out his walking powers. Bully Forrester, holding his jaw in bewildered fashion, hoisted himself through the hatch, and saw him.

"Skipper's waitin' for you aft, my bully," he snarled. "Just you cut along, now! When Steelfist Charley's through with you, I'll 'tend to anything else you want — if you want any more."

Blake laughed, a trifle shakily. Shanghaied! He had read about it, of course, but it "wasn't done" now, according to books. Anyway, he knew his rights as a citizen.

"If this man Marshall overpowers me, weak as I am," thought Jack, "he can't hold me when we make port. In the meantime, he'll learn that he has Jack Blake aboard, that's sure!"

Quite unconscious of the absurd figure which he presented, Blake marched resolutely along the heaving deck, Forrester following him, and climbed the poop ladder; at the top, Blake made out a vaguely familiar shape standing on the weather side, abreast of the wheel.

All the happenings of the previous evening surged back into his mind at sight of that tremendous figure.

Crisp black curls, glittering eyes — albeit one was now surrounded by a purple ring — long arms, and black gloves; the same wolfish expression which, fastened on that girl, had first drawn Blake's attention — there was no room for doubt. This skipper and the girl's assailant were one and the same person!

With double outrage burning in him, Blake strode toward this grim giant. Under the bushy brows, the glittering eyes seemed more sunken than ever, but glowed with lurid fires. The thin lips drew back from yellow, irregular fangs as Blake planted himself squarely before the skipper.

"Confound you for a pirate!" he broke out furiously. "I demand that you set me ashore at once!"

Steelfist Marshall raised his brows. The corners of his mouth disappeared in wrinkles of hard muscle. He nodded to the mate, who edged up behind Blake.

"Did you ship a waiter for the seamen, Mr. Forrester?" drawled the skipper in slow sarcasm. "I hate dirty waiters. You might's well rig the head pump and wash him off before you bring him aft again."

Bully Forrester grinned appreciation. He sidled alongside Blake, an ebony fid gripped in his big fist.

"I'm no waiter for your hog-pen, and you know it," shot back Blake, his fists clenched. "I'm not one of your filthy sailors, and unless you set me ashore at once, I can promise you a mighty unpleasant voyage —"

"Consarn you, keep your eyes on that compass!" stormed the skipper, whirling on the helmsman, who was grinning at Blake's scarecrow apparel. "Mr. Forrester, are you going to take this flunkey to the pump, or do I have to take him myself?"

Blake, maddened, wasted no more time in talk. He forgot the manifold aches and pains that burned his head and body and slid close in with a neat shift which frustrated the mate's pleasant intention to trip him.

One fierce lead he landed square on Marshall's sneering mouth — then he was shaken to the heels by a terrific right counter that made his ribs crack. It was the same bone-crushing right which had beaten him down in the fog by the Custom House.

Blake's seething rage blotted that memory from his mind. He only saw his grinning enemy, the grin demoniacal by reason of the blood his first blow had drawn; flinging overboard all his knowledge of boxing, he rushed in wildly.

Something fell across his legs, a splitting crack descended over his ear, and that terrible right fist of the skipper's thudded to his cheek, cutting the flesh to the bone and hurling him bodily into the poop rail.

After that, all was blank.

Under the application of cold salt water that gushed burstingly from the nozzle of a pump and soaked him thoroughly, Jack Blake came to himself.

The sting of the brine on his cut cheek was maddening. His eyes smarted with the salt. Groaning, he rolled away from the merciless stream.

A watery gleam of daylight touched his swollen face and he struggled into a sitting posture, trying to see out of his puffed and burning eyes. The voice of the mate sounded from somewhere near.

"Dump him below an' pull them rags off him. One o' you lend him some dungarees. If he kicks, whale him!"

In the foul-smelling fo'c's'le again, Blake groped his way to a bunk and collapsed. His brain was in a chaotic state, and he could pay little heed to what passed around him.

The watch had just come below and breakfast was in progress; the gloomy den was filled with the odors of humanity and bilge water. One of the men slipped over to Blake and offered him a tin pannikin of steaming coffee.

"Here, matey," he said, not unkindly, "take a swig on this! It'll put some guts into ye, and nex' time ye plaster that cow-son aft I hope ye crack his bloody sky-piece!"

With a muttered word of thanks, Blake took the pannikin. He tasted the scalding stuff and squirmed inwardly. Coffee! If this was coffee, he had fooled himself all his life!

But it was hot and reasonably sweetened with black molasses. After a sip or two his inner man responded to its warmth, and he found himself listening to the uncouth noises that passed for table talk among the half-dozen men. His friend of the coffee, whom the others called Paddy Ryan, seemed to be watching him, and promptly came over again when Blake showed signs of interest in life.

Ryan was a small man, very wrinkled, but with efficiency stamped in his whole bearing. Blake felt instinctively that here was a friend, and one who was able to help him find himself in this new environment.

If Jack Blake had ever been tainted with snobbishness, it was clean wiped out of him by this time. He met Ryan's cheery grin with a faint smile.

"See here, matey," began Paddy, "you ain't one of us, that's plain.

But you're here, an' here you'll have to be stoppin' till this ship gets some'eres. So you might as well eat some grub. You ain't goin' to lick Steelfist Charley half starved, me bully boy!"

Once the coffee had put a warm glow beneath his belt, the same thought had come to Blake himself. He realized exactly how matters stood. He knew that if he did not at least make a show of accepting his lot, the entire after-guard of the ship would beat him mercilessly until he did.

Having eaten nothing since the previous evening, he was hungry. Determined to conquer that skipper with the terrible right, he resolved to store away strength. And finally, being very much of a man, he resolved that he would never sign articles or in any shape give up his rights under the law.

He came to his feet with another faint smile.

"Hold on," exclaimed Ryan, reaching down a bundle from his own bunk, just opposite. "Peel them glad duds, matey! Put 'em in yer bunk — 'tis all the beddin' ye get. And you can use these here slops o' mine till you sign on an' do be gettin' some more from the slop-chest."

The "slops" were a pair of dungaree trousers and a jacket of the same stuff; not new, not too clean, but certainly more in keeping with the surroundings than his evening clothes, thought Blake. He put them on grimly and took a place at the mess kids.

Being too sore to converse, Blake silently gnawed a scrap of hardtack and endeavored to wash it down with drafts of coffee. Then he discovered that, when the coffee became cool enough to drink readily, it also developed a taste which he could not stomach.

Hard though he tried, he found it impossible to down that coffee. He was not at all seasick. As a boy, Blake had made many cruises in his father's yacht, and had become well acquainted with sea life — from the other end of the ship. This was something new, however.

Giving up the effort, he bethought himself to search his pockets. When he left the club, he had had something over a hundred dollars in gold. Now he found himself stripped of money and valuables, save for one ten-dollar gold piece in a vest pocket.

Searching his bunk, he found a cranny in the sheathing and slipped the gold piece into it. Later, he thought, it might come in useful, and it would certainly be confiscated by officers or stolen by his shipmates did it appear in his possession.

From a scuttle-butt beneath the ladder, Blake now obtained a pannikin of water, which proved better than the coffee. While he munched his biscuit with its help, the little hatch was darkened by a descending figure; a square, muscular, bronzed seaman dropped down and took his seat on a vacant sea chest.

This proved to be the bo'sun, Fancy Harry Lovell, snatching a surreptitious smoke below. His pipe was soon going, and at once a rumble of growls buzzed from all quarters. Fancy Harry was one man to whom the fo'c's'le might grumble and still know that their complaints would carry no farther.

"Hey, Fancy! What kind o' grub's this?" sang out a big hulk of a man. "Dawg biscuit an' bootleg! I signed for beef, didn't I?"

"How the blazes do you know what you signed for, Keough?" grinned the bo'sun complacently. "It took four men to h'ist you over the rail, and both mates an' me to get you up to the windlass. Shut your head! You'll get used to this grub afore we reach Sydney Heads!"

At this, Blake raised his head and looked steadily at Lovell.

"Sydney, did you say? Are we bound for Sydney?"

"Why, damme if it ain't the dude!" exclaimed Fancy Harry.

To Blake's surprise he extended a hairy paw covered with tattooed stars and anchors.

"Put her thar, matey! I've sailed with Steelfist three year now, allus hoping to see him get what you gave him. Shake!"

Those who had seen Blake's interview with the skipper lost no time in passing the word around. The fo'c's'le shook with deep-sea voices lifted in rude appreciation and incredulous query:

"You the guy what plastered the Ol' Man in the gob?"

"An' give him a shiner?"

"An' smeared his ugly face like a pudden?"

Blake looked from face to face, wondering inwardly. From his own point of view, he had failed ignominiously and wished only to be rid of the subject. Yet, despite his new nickname of "The Dude," he seemed to command respect among these men.

And, suddenly realizing this, he laughed and flung back his shoulders.

"Sure," he nodded response, "And I'm going to do it again, mates. Lovell, when do we get to Sydney?"

CHAPTER III

THE PUNISHMENT

Fancy Harry Lovell was a Job's comforter.

"Can't say, matey," he responded slowly, to Blake's query. "Don't know that we're goin' to Sydney. Cap'n Marshall goes where he likes, mostly, an' does worse. But you can bet you're booked for six months — hey, where you bound for?"

The bo'sun reached out and clamped strong fingers on Blake, as the latter rose with a grunt.

"Where? I'm going to go see that pirate again —"

"Easy, now easy!" advised Lovell softly. "You ain't got a chance against Steelfist an' the mates, let alone the big Chink! Easy, matey; you're too good a man to see slaughtered by the skipper's steel fist."

Blake halted, staring at the other in surprise.

"What's this about a steel fist?" he queried.

A grin passed around the faces.

"Thought you'd found out," returned the bo'sun. "You been up against it twice. The Old Man's got a steel fist — that's no lie! He lost his right paw through meddlin' with a cook who could use a cleaver. New he's got a fist of steel, padded to the stump an' laced up his arm to the elbow. What d'ye think he wears them gloves for?"

Blake nodded and turned to his bunk.

"You're right, bo'sun," he said simply. "I'll wait."

"Yes," said a voice, amid silence from the others. "An' we'll be wid ye, matey!"

A steel hand, eh? Jack Blake remembered those awful right swings, and no longer wondered at how he had gone to sleep under them.

As he sat there staring at the floor he did not realize that more than one of the men followed Lovell's eyes to his face with something like admiration.

Blake was not good to look upon in that moment, but something in him was being slowly brought to the surface — something which had long been hidden under luxurious ease and the lazy enjoyment of wealth. It was not for Jack Blake's eyes to see, however.

Whither was all this leading, he thought? Misery, squalor, brutality! Why had he been pitchforked into it — as ironic reward for championing a girl?

Ah, the girl! What had become of her? Where was she? Into and out of his life had she drifted, and this was the aftermath — his burden.

To these reflections he was left until the afternoon watch, when the skipper summoned him to sign on the articles. Such abject capitulation was quite opposite to his intentions, and it was with hard-set jaw that he faced Steelfist Marshall in the little saloon cabin.

Forrester had the deck. The second mate, Long Rube Bower, a lanky, pockmarked ruffian, who chewed steadily at monstrous quids, stood at the captain's elbow. Near Blake's shoulder hovered the steward, the largest Chinaman he had ever seen.

"What's your name?" snapped Marshall wolfishly.

"You'll discover that at our first port," said Blake steadily, giving look for look. "I'll —"

"You'll sign on as Ordinary Seaman, at ten dollars a month, and you'll keep your watch on deck with the other rats —"

"Confound you," broke in Blake angrily, "I'll do nothing of the kind!"

"I will now read you the articles —" began Marshall.

But the articles were omitted at that interview, for Blake's rage overtopped his caution and he rushed.

As he did so, however, the long arms of the steward encircled him from behind and grappled him in a hug that made arms and ribs crack together. In the same instant the second mate reached out a pair of claws like grappling arms and twisted them in a choking grip about the American's neck.

Flung to the cabin floor, he was wrenched over on his face and felt the iron of handcuffs closing on his wrists. His legs were lashed with small rope. Then Bower rolled him over with an ungentle foot and squirted a stream of tobacco juice into his face.

"Those who won't work won't eat," remarked Captain Marshall. "Mr. Bower, find a soft spot in the chain locker. Don't mishandle him — more than usual. He won't appreciate punishment for assaulting his commander, yet a while. Treat him gently; I'll punish him later."

At a sign from Bower the Chinaman seized the ropes confining Blake's legs and marched up the companionway dragging Blake as he would a sack of coal.

Striking each brassbound step with his head, while the handcuffs tore the skin from his wrists as they hitched under the steps, Blake soon lost all sense of separate pains. His whole body burned and tingled in one tremendous bruise; his brain went numb under the torture.

Across the poop deck and down the short ladder — there were six steps, as Blake dimly remembered afterward — then the long stretch of the main deck, dry and hot under the sun which had appeared toward noon. So they came to the fo'c's'le hatch.

"Stand from under!" barked Bower and dropped his prisoner headlong.

The chain-locker hatch abaft the heel of the bowsprit was lifted, and, with no "stand from under" this time, Blake was bundled through the hole, to fall with a crash on the piled chain cables. Then the hatch was replaced.

Here was torture such as Blake had never in his life dreamed or read of. Painfully squirming until he found the middle of the range of chain, he composed himself in bitterness of spirit and body, amid the deafening clatter of chain-links.

The air was poisonous, his lungs were clogged as though with ashes. With every leeward lean of the ship the bilge water, compounded from salt water and drainings of the last cargo of raw sugar, erupted a stench that would have turned the stomach of a Hottentot. Each lurch of the vessel flung poor Blake into the tiers of chain with sickening force.

How long he lay here he never knew. He was in a half stupor of abject misery and anguish when the hatch was lifted and a man dropped cautiously beside him.

"Where are ye, matey?" whispered a hoarse voice. "It's me, Paddy Ryan!"

Blake felt kind, groping hands at his head. Ryan's arm came beneath him, lifting his face from the chains.

"Here, take a swig on this, matey —"and Blake felt the neck of a bottle at his lips. "'Tis good stuff, for I did be swipin' it from the stooard's locker. Tokay, ses the label."

Jack Blake managed to swallow a mouthful, chokingly. The fire of the wine crept through his veins and gave stimulance to his outraged body and restored his nerves to some semblance of strength.

"I dassn't let ye loose," lamented Paddy Ryan, "it'd only make 'em use ye worser. But here's a hunk o' horse. Chaw on it an' ye'll feel better, mebbe."

For a moment Blake bit hungrily into the piece of salt, hard beef that was poked at his mouth. It softened under his teeth, but he felt too ill to continue.

"You're mighty good, Ryan," he muttered thickly. "How long will they keep me like this?"

"Till you're ready to sign on, I reckon. They'll ask ye in the mornin'. I heard Steelfist say ye'd be gettin' no grub till ye signed."

Paddy folded up his dungaree jumper and placed it beneath Blake's neck. Then he continued:

"Ye'd better sign, matey. Ye can't get even down here, and ye'll starve afore them swine lets up on ye. Steelfist is the mother an' father of Ol' Nick! He's got the big Dutchman an' young Boston triced up by the thumbs to the sheer-pole all the dog watch, 'cause they looked sideways at Long Rube when he dragged ye for'ard."

"But if I sign," objected Blake, his stubborn spirit rising anew, "can't they jail me if I skip the ship?"

"If ye don't sign they'll starve ye. Ain't a man in the crowd as don't want to see ye lam the everlastin' halleluyer out o' them bloody officers, matey! Ses I, you're too good a man to feed the rats in a stinkin' windjammer's chain locker. There's me an' Fancy Harry, an' Cutlip Sullivan, an' big Frank Keough, an' others, as has waited a year and more for the chance to ship together with Steelfist."

"We're goin' to snatch the chance, while we got it! Wait till we hit the tirades, an' our nose is lookin' a bit furder from California! We'll get Marshall an' his bucko mates, an' the yeller ape of a stooard — we'll get 'em, an' ye'll be enjoyin' the sport. Make up your mind to sign, see?"

Paddy returned as he had come, leaving Jack Blake a sadder but wiser man.

Through the long night of horror that followed the shanghaied millionaire bent all his energies to keeping back the groans that rose to his lips. Every link of cable was a red-hot devil gnawing into his flesh; every lee lurch of the ship tumbled the chain about him, until his flesh was raw where the jamming links had nipped it.

Yet, through the night Blake's mind reverted to the face of the girl whom he had seen in the light of the post office doorway — was it ages ago, or only the previous evening?

Why had Steelfist Marshall been following her? The question drummed insistently at his brain. Not because she was a woman, certainly; the snatch of talk which he had overheard proved that Marshall had had more serious purposes in view. Apparently he had tried to force the girl to charter the *C. H. Marshall* — but why?

Blake fell into an agonized sleep, still wondering.

In the forenoon watch, Bully Forrester shoved his rugged head down the hatch and hailed the captive gruffly.

"Now, my blooming swell, d'you want to sign? Answer sharp!"

"Yes, for God's sake take me out of this!" replied Blake weakly. "I'll sign."

Casting the lashings from his legs, but not removing the wrist irons, Forrester marched Blake up the ladder and aft to the cabin. Stumbling from cramp and weariness, his head swimming and his eyes aching drearily, Blake found himself once more facing the wolf-eyed skipper.

"Want me to read the articles?" asked Marshall grimly.

"No," and Blake gripped the table for support. "Give me a pen — let me go."

Thus Jack Blake entered upon his duties as Ordinary Seaman of the full-rigged ship *C. H. Marshall*. He was placed in the mate's watch, and for the rest of the forenoon went about like a man in a fog, driven to his work.

Eight bells clanged barely in time to save him from utter collapse. He stumbled below, found the bunk where his tattered dress-clothes were stowed, and rolled in to get what relief he could from his bed of sailor's feathers — hard deal plank.

He was asleep before the mess kids arrived from the galley.

This was the last meal that Blake missed for some time, however. He wakened from his heavy sleep greatly refreshed in body and mind; what was better, his head had cooled. He said "sir" to Bully Forrester and did what was given him to do; behind his grimly clenched lips he kept in mind the one word — wait!

For several days he was left in peace. Thanks to Paddy Ryan, he soon learned his way about the ship's rigging, while he rapidly regained his old clearness of eye and springiness of step.

It was Paddy, too, who shared "whacks" with him; thus, in the days of his novitiate, assuring him a fair share of fat with his beef and lean with his pork, neither of which he could have wrested alone from the tarry talons of the shellbacks. His first acquaintance, Cutlip Sullivan, developed an undisguised aversion for him.

Thus, as the ship edged southward through an unbroken sea of long, lazy swells, Jack Blake found himself fitting into his new role. And, except when he allowed himself to brood upon his own case, he found much to admire in this new life.

The morning wash down, for example, was a fit opening for any man's day. In the crisp sunrise, when the ocean slowly emerged from its night-robe of black velvet and diamond stars to reveal itself bare and unblushing in shimmery blue, the sparkling gush from the head-pump was a direct challenge to laziness.

Buckets of water flew every way; if a man caught one of them, what matter? He was the better for the wash!

But fine weather in the *C. H. Marshall* gave her men too many chances for growling, and Blake began to see other things.

He saw "Big Frank" Keough laid on his back on the fore-hatch, hands and feet stretched with small line to each corner; he saw Long Rube Bower throw bucket after bucket of water over the prone figure; he saw the rope, new and hard and already drawn taut, tighten with the repeated wetting and pull Keough four ways at once, until the man screamed in horrible agony.

He saw young Boston, as a penalty for bad steering, hung by the thumbs to the mizzen-stay, his feet eighteen inches from the deck. He saw Steelfist Marshall hang a holystone to each boot "to make him swing regular," until the lad's terrible shrieks had died down to still more terrible groans.

On the second day after picking up the northeast trades, when the ship was clothed from chesstree to dog-vanes with pearly canvas, Blake was summoned by the mate.

"Lay aft here — cap'n wants you. Remember that little matter of assault that ain't been cleared up? Lay aft, you swine — shake a leg, there!"

Blake looked into Forrester's hard, leering eyes. Then he turned toward the cabin, feeling as though a cold hand had gripped on his heart.

He caught a mute glance of helpless entreaty from Paddy Ryan, at the helm, and the warning look restored his self-control. He went below, smoldering fire in his gray eyes, but his long jaw gripped hard in restraint.

Captain Marshall sat at the table in his little saloon, the logbook before him. At his shoulder stood Rube Bower, champing at a great plug. The huge Chinese steward was hovering in the background.

"John Blake," said the skipper, his voice like chilled steel, "some time ago you attempted a violent and unwarranted assault on your commander. I have here the entry of the circumstance, attested by Mr. Bower. You seemed not to be strong and were not punished at the time; but I cannot allow such offenses to go unnoticed. As you have seen, my ship is ruled by kind but firm discipline. You will now submit to such punishment as Mr. Bower feels will suit the case. Take him away, Mr. Bower."

This amazing pronouncement drew nothing from Blake save a steady gaze. His gray eyes bit into Marshall's gaze like gimlets; then, without a word, he turned and followed the second mate on deck.

Long Rube turned to a nearby seaman.

"Hey, you! Lay out on the lee main yardarm an' take a tail-block with you! Reeve a heavin' line and give me both ends. Lively, now!"

Without a word of warning, he flung himself on Blake, assisted by the Chinese steward. Before the American could get in a blow he was trussed up and lying face down on the deck, his hands lashed to his ankles behind him.

The line was passed down from the yardarm and one end made fast to Blake's lashed wrists and ankles. Then he heard the second mate sing out; the steward tallied on, and Blake felt himself rising, bumping over the bulwarks, finally to swing clear.

Under him was the heaving sea.

His head struck the lee leach of the mainsail, and he spun like a spider at the end of a line. Then he swung back, felt the line running out — and plunged into the churned-up waters under the lee rail.

The line tautened with the drag of the ship. Blake felt every muscle in his legs, arms and body crack with the strain, as his hollowed back surged against the water. Hands and feet near to bursting with the compress of the line, half suffocated, he was slowly dragged up — up — up until his body touched the block at the end of the yard.

The grim laughter of the mates rang in his ears. With a thrill of horror he saw himself going down at the green water again, and he wanted to scream out. But his lips tightened — and he did not scream, then or afterward.

Five times was this repeated — five times he was hoisted to the block, five times swung down to drag in the water alongside.

"I think that's enough, Mr. Bower," said the cold voice of Marshall.

Blake, half dead, was pulled in. He was jerked to his feet before the skipper, who eyed him with that wolfish snarl which Blake hated with all his heart and soul.

"Take care, Blake, that you don't repeat your fault. I'll have to punish you severely the next time. Go for'ard."

It was three days before he could again stand his watch.

CHAPTER IV

A PROPOSITION FROM STEELFIST

During those days of agony, it was Paddy Ryan who stole grease from the galley to rub Blake's chafed limbs, and who filched a roast fowl from the pantry through the main deck port, when Blake could not look at salt beef.

Paddy took his life in his hands to perform these acts of kindness, and Jack Blake was well aware of the fact.

When the pain wore off, Blake recovered rapidly from the punishment. When mealtime came along, he was soon ready to take his place at the grimy mess kids, and to scramble for his share, and many were the rough jests passed over the remaking of the Dude.

With these Blake put up good naturedly, until Cutlip Sullivan put too much of an edge into his japes. Cutlip, in common with some of the others, took for granted that the "Old Man" had effectually smashed the Dude's spirit; and on one occasion allowed his personalities to become altogether too pointed.

The result was astonishing — to Cutlip Sullivan. Blake, very cool and sure of himself, blinded the other man with cutting straight drives; when Cutlip sent his bullet-head driving for the stomach, Blake stepped aside and planted a neat short-arm jolt to the temple.

Cutlip fell with a crash over the hawse-pipe and stayed there.

"Flap yer wings an' crow!" advised some one.

Blake, untouched, only smiled. That encounter did him good — made him sure of himself again. Also, it gave him a definite status which admitted him to the circle of deepwater men.

Thus, when both watches were gathered on the fo'c's'le head in the dog-watches, and Blake was busily picking out the bunt-lines, clewlines, leachlines, halliards and braces, in comparison with a list given him by Paddy Ryan for his guidance, Fancy Harry Lovell came and desired his presence with the crowd.

"We'll pull off a stunt tonight, Dude," said the bo'sun quietly. "You won't kick at getting a chance at Steelfist on level terms, will you?"

"Not a bit," smiled Blake promptly, and Fancy Harry nodded at the steady gray eyes of him. "I'm not crazy any more, though. Let me get him but of reach of the big Chink and the mates —"

"We'll 'tend to *them*," rumbled Big Frank Keough, amid a growl of assent. "If you can fix Steelfist, we'll do the rest!"

Blake glanced around cautiously. Paddy Ryan had the wheel, Marshall and Rube Bower stood together at the poop rail, and the mate was stumping back and forth on the weather side. For a moment Blake forgot what was going on, as he looked up.

With the strong breeze pouring over her starboard quarter, the ship heeled easily with a throbbing hum and boom of canvas and rigging. The towering square-sails, mounting from the great arch of the courses to the quivering royals, were suffused with the tints of mother-o'-pearl by the setting sun over the weather bow.

"Listen, Dude —" the bo'sun's voice called Blake to attention. "You've seen what kind o' sweet angels we got to knuckle under to! You've had their 'tentions too, though at that I ain't so sure that they got much change out o' you.

"Now, we signed on for a Sydney voyage. We could lay our course with this wind, but we ain't headin' that way by a handful o' points; Steelfist is up to his tricks, see? Gawd knows where we're goin'!"

"We're not heading for Sydney?" inquired Blake sharply. "Sure?"

The other nodded quietly, one eye on the poop.

"You come along with us at eight bells, and we'll ask the skipper where he's bound for. He'll slam the man that asks him, but he won't get a chance at his gun — we'll pile onto him an' them sweet mates, an' give 'em holy Hades. How 'bout it?"

"Eh? Mutiny?" The word was not nice to Blake's notion of things. "We —"

"Not by a jugful," dissented Fancy Harry hastily. "Not us! We'll lick Steelfist an' the mates, see — lick the livin' guts out of 'em. We signed on for Sydney, but they ain't takin' us there, see? If they lick us silly, we lose, o' course. If we lick them, they got to let up on the crew. They can't put us all in irons or they couldn't work ship. See?"

Blake nodded thoughtfully, appreciating this deepwater logic. The officers, in order to work ship, would have to keep hands off the crew. There might be a settling at port, and the officers might not be whipped; those chances would have to be taken.

"I'm with you," he said quietly, realizing that they looked to him to handle the terrible skipper. "Take care of the mates — I'll rough it with Steelfist."

"Good. Hang about the waist-end o' the second dog-watch. Eight bells starts it."

When relieving Paddy Ryan at the helm Blake mentioned the proposed scheme. The Irishman's wrinkled, broad face creased up earnestly.

"Did the bo'sun say we'd do 'em up proper, matey?"

"All hands in it, Paddy."

"Elegant!" grinned Paddy Ryan. "Then don't be makin' no mistake when ye slam the Ol' Man — leave the rest to us!"

When eight bells echoed along the shadowy decks, the sound jumping from sail to sail and dying away to leeward, Blake was waiting beneath the weather poop ladder. At the bell, he saw flitting figures swarming aft and slipped up the ladder. He reached the poop just as a crowd poured up the lee ladder, and he started toward the companionway slide.

Then came a sudden hesitation — a silence. The poop was dark, save when the bows soared high, at which times the rising moon sent a patch of light athwart the deck. Blake looked around, saw the men halted by the mizzenmast.

The moon, just above the horizon, cast a widening path of violet and gold, silver-gray and black, straight into the ship's wake. It ruled the lee leaches of the mizzen in glaring lines of luminous light, leaving sharp contrasting shadows stretched from lee-earing to weather-clew.

In that brief pause, the bows rose high on a swell, and moonlight flooded the poop; with it came the skipper, rising through the companionway. His eye caught Blake's figure, and his snarling voice ripped through the night.

"Mr. Bower! You doped — What the —" Bower, who had not seen the advancing men, swung around with an oath. Blake paid no heed to him, but marched forward to the skipper, the men crowding behind.

"I want to know where this ship is going, sir," he said quietly, balancing lightly to the swing of the deck, and keeping a wary eye on the skipper's deadly right.

Marshall had left the companionway. Now, seeing the men crowding around, he turned with an oath.

"Forrester! Stooard! Bring your guns!"

In the same breath, he swung straight for Blake's jaw. As he slipped the blow, Blake heard a low growl and saw the lanky figure of Long Rube Bower flailing blows upon a host of foes.

With a deep breath of relief and savage joy, Blake met the skipper's rush. They were on even terms, now that he knew the secret of that steel hand; he kept clear of it carefully, sliding in and out with machine-like rhythm, and shooting in stinging blows that made the skipper grunt.

He dimly heard the rush of the mate and steward up the companionway, and a shot rang out somewhere. Then came a second low growl of maddened men, and the crew closed in on both mates and the big Chinaman.

Cutlip, at the wheel, deserted his post and slipped into the crowd. At that instant Blake saw the motion; also, he saw the gleam of steel in Sullivan's hand. A mad fear surged through him at thought of what would happen once murder was done.

Desperate to get into the mêlée and stop Sullivan, he turned on Marshall with a savage fury at this beast who had made murder possible. A swing of that iron hand whistled over his shoulder; with rigid arm, whirled round by the full weight of his body, Blake brought the edge of his own right hand like lightning to the skipper's throat.

The blow caught Marshall fair on his Adam's apple. One gasp, and the skipper sank to his knees, emitting a weird sound as he half strangled under the blow. His eyes bulged, his mouth gaped like that of a gasping codfish, and he went limp.

Leaving Marshall where he lay, Blake hurled himself into the crowd of struggling men.

The Chinese steward had gone down, insensible under the trampling feet. Long Rube Bower had been tossed over the stern, but was towing by a line. Bully Forrester backed against the rail, stood with the bo'sun gripping his revolver hand. His left was locked about the wrist of Cutlip Sullivan; blows were raining upon him, but Forrester hung on grimly.

"See to the ship, bo'sun!" commanded Blake sharply, flinging aside the men.

A thunderous rattle and rapping aloft told of the ship rounding into the wind. Blake gripped Forrester's revolver and tore it away; Fancy Harry leaped to the helm, leaving Blake, Forrester and Cutlip Sullivan locked together.

"Hands to th' braces! Lively, for Gawd's sake!" yelled the bo'sun.

Most of the crowd melted away to secure the ship, for immediate action was imperative. Blake gripped Cutlip's arm.

"Down with that knife, you fool!" he ordered.

Sullivan turned a face twisted with rage and madness.

"Go to Hades!" he snapped back furiously.

Having already secured a half-Nelson on Cutlip's free arm, Blake promptly put it into play. The man went to his knees with a bellow of pain. Instantly Bully Forrester had gripped him by the throat with both hands, a snarling oath on his lips.

Blake stepped back. Again he brought the edge of his palm to the throat of a man — the blow caught Forrester fair and square. With a gurgling gasp the mate slid down, caught at the bulwarks and went limp.

"Get forward, Sullivan!" commanded Blake swiftly and sped the fellow with a blow. Then he leaped to the rail, where Paddy Ryan was hauling in the second mate, and in two moments had Bower spouting water like a picture-book whale.

At a touch, Blake turned to find Fancy Harry at his elbow, anxious of face.

"What's to do, Dude?"

"Suit yourself," and Blake laughed grimly. He patted Forrester's revolver, which he had slipped into his pocket. "Want to put 'em in irons?"

"No — we dassn't mutiny," returned the bo'sun.

Marshall and his mate lay on the deck, staring goggle-eyed at the moon while the men examined them none too gently, wondering at the efficacy of the Dude. Bower was in no shape to fight further, and Fancy Harry called the men around him.

Big Frank Keough was something of a sea-lawyer and threshed out the situation.

Marshall had attacked Blake wantonly and had struck the first blow. If things were left *in statu quo*, the officers would have learned their lesson; if they were ironed and deprived of command, it was mutiny.

"All right," nodded Blake, taking things in charge. "We'll have no mutiny, of course. We've done what we started to do, so let it end there. Keep an eye on Sullivan, Keough, or he'll use that knife of his. Break up, men."

With the bo'sun he approached Bower.

"Mr. Bower, the ship's in your hands. You are a witness that Cap'n Marshall struck the first blow."

And in this fashion ended the amazing battle on the *C. H. Marshall*.

Days of uneasiness followed; days when the ocean slid and writhed in long, greasy hillocks and hollows, the ship's wake swirling with oily bubbles. The fo'c's'le was uneasy, for no word came from aft.

Nothing was said by the skipper. No one was triced up and flogged. No mention of the fight was made by either skipper or mates. It was so uncanny, so contrary to custom on this hellship, that the uneasiness in the fo'c's'le grew more painful at each watch.

Jack Blake discovered a still more painful thing, however — he had made no friends forward when he had saved Forrester from the knife of Cutlip Sullivan. In proportion as the men grew more afraid of Marshall's grim, cryptic smile, they regretted not having killed the two mates and mutinied. Even Paddy Ryan evinced a reserve that surprised Blake.

"Paddy, what's the mystery about?" he asked one night. "The ship feels like the roof of a burning powder mill, and you boys seem to think I set it alight!"

"Ain't no mystery, Dude," returned Paddy moodily. "The crowd's markin' time to see what Steelfist's got in his ugly head. What in thunder did you turn around an' queer the game for, Dude? The crowd's sore as a boil!"

Blake's gray eyes narrowed half angrily.

"I stopped murder, Paddy. I joined in for a scrap and had it. I didn't look for knife-play and sha'n't assist it without justification."

Ryan's face darkened in disgust, and he spat savagely over the rail.

"Justification — hell! Ain't ye seen enough o' that aboard this hooker? That ain't murder — it's jest fair come-back. Mark this, Dude — Steelfist is goin' to cut loose, an' if he goes to beat us up or put the bracelets on us, there'll be murder an' ye won't stop it."

"You think he won't let the thing drop?"

"Who — him? Mebbe he will, Dude, mebbe he will. If he does, Gawd help ye! I'm your friend, but there's mighty few more."

Blake did not understand this at all, but came to a fuller comprehension that same evening. And when he did, he saw that Paddy Ryan had been a wise prophet.

All through the first dogwatch, the old hands sniffed at the wind, pointed out the increasing frequency with which the long swells broke into froth, and peered under the sharp of a hand at a low, ragged white vapor down in the western quadrant of the heaving circle of sea. As the skipper appeared on deck after supper, Forrester let out a bellow.

"Muster aft, all hands!"

Muttering, conjecturing, growling doubtfully, the fo'c's'le rats trooped along the main deck and clustered at the break of the poop. Leaning on the rail, the skipper and both mates regarded the seamen keenly.

Blake stood at one side, with Paddy Ryan and the bo'sun.

"Wondering why you haven't all been flaked, I s'pose?" began the steely voice of Marshall, his wolfish eyes resting on Blake. "I'll tell you. It ain't too late yet to put you through the hoops for that piece o' fun you had. But I got better work for fine men o' spirit like you; if you're all of a mind I may forget that night — it's up to you."

With this prelude, Marshall took a turn aft and peeped at the compass. Then he resumed, after a long look ahead.

"Wanted to know where I'm bound for, didn't you, *Mister* Blake?" The sarcasm in his cold voice boded trouble. "That's up to you too, men. Under that cloud ahead is Oahu — Makapuu Point. If you say so, you'll see Honolulu tomorrow. There's a ship in there that's after something which belongs to me. Now, you're all first-class fighting men, ain't you?"

The two mates broke into a hoarse laugh. The men below shifted uneasily.

"If you want to row in with me an' help get what's mine anyway, you can have all the fightin' you want without murderin' your officers. You'll stand a chance o' puttin' a wad of money in your belts to boot."

Marshall paused. Fancy Harry stepped to the front, boldly enough.

"Tell us the hoodie, cap'n. Some o' your games ain't healthy."

The skipper's eyes glinted, and hard wrinkles played about his thin lips.

"My games ain't healthy for the man who queers them, Lovell. You can stay out if you're scared. Because you may get cold feet, I'll not say where we're bound for till we leave Diamond Head behind, but this I will say. There's 'bout half a ton o' coin belonging to me that's sunk in a lagoon not a million miles from here, and I'm after it. It ain't a secret, and others is after it too. That's why I want you bold lads to row in with me."

"What if we don't, sir?" growled Cutlip Sullivan.

"Just this, my bully. There's a fine jail in Honolulu. Get me?"

It was evident that the men "got" him. There was a little rumble of voices, Blake being patently disregarded. Looking up, Blake saw the eyes of the skipper fastened on him with a venomous intensity.

"Well, bullies — what's the answer?"

"We're in, cap'n," cried Sullivan. "But we ain't goin' to pull with the Dude — he's a welsher, he is!"

The skipper slipped a hand into his pocket. Too late, Blake was mindful of the revolver which he had hidden in a cranny of his fo'c's'le bunk along with his gold piece.

"Right and proper!" snapped Marshall. "Lay into him, bullies, and tie him up! The lazarette's open!"

Before Blake quite sensed that trouble was on him, Long Rube Bower had vaulted over the rail and borne him down. Forrester and Sullivan joined in on the instant; Blake was overpowered, crushed to the deck, and trussed up.

Five minutes later he lay in the stuffy little storeroom beneath the cabin, the sting of Marshall's kicks still on his ribs.

CHAPTER V

FOOL OR KNIGHT?

As at a tremendous distance, Blake heard the ship's bell clang faintly.

Eight bells — then one — two — three — then four bells, ten o'clock at night. Immediately after the last stroke the sounds of shortening sail came down to him, and he knew that the ship had come up with the land.

Soon, above the squeaking and shrilling of chafing cases and barrels around him, the grind of tiller-tackles and thump of rudder jarred on his ears. Then the rhythmic, sliding motion told him that the ship was hove-to under topsails for the night.

Suddenly he heard voices above him, in the cabin.

"Might's well let up on the Dude, cap'n," rumbled the deep bass of Bully Forrester. "If it hadn't been for him, Rube'd be shark bait and I'd have a knife in my gizzard. Dunno where *you'd* ha' been!"

"Fire it out of your fat head," retorted the skipper icily. "You think I loaded him aboard 'cause o' that black eye? Not me — though it's against my religion to take a shiner off a silk-hat dude without slapping him on the wrist for it. Listen!"

The captain's voice dropped, but the words filtered down to Blake nevertheless.

"That patched t'gallants'l that slipped into port just before we hove to — you've seen her before? That's the *John Foster*. What's she doin' here? Why, what we would be doin', only for that meddlin' dude!

"You've heard about ol' Cap'n Peabody, him what made a pile in the Sydney trade when it was good? Well, his granddaughter has the right dope where his ship was laid up, with every darned cent he made, on the passage home to 'Frisco. No banks for ol' Peabody — he kep' a strongbox in his cabin!"

Forrester broke in with a startled oath. Marshall continued.

"The girl's chartered the *Foster* to get it. I'd have got the job — had the girl dead to rights that last night in 'Frisco, when the damned Dude chipped in an' spoiled the game. If I let him get away, he'll crab my deal, see? Some o' the *Foster*'s people would find out from him that I was the man who talked to the girl that night — you see, she didn't know me from Adam, an' they won't suspect what we're after."

"Well, what are we after?" growled the mate. "What we puttin' in here for?"

"To get a line on the *Foster*, you fool! We got to get one of her crew, or the girl herself if we can, an' find out just where she's bound."

"Can't we heave the Dude overboard when we leave?" asked the mate, who had evidently been appreciative of Blake's action.

"No — I got a notion that we may need to use him first. Leave him lay."

The voices ceased. Every tiny protesting whimper of the ship's frame filled the ensuing silence.

So — this was the game! Blake, staring into the darkness, thrilled to the outline of the story as he pieced it together.

That girl, the rightful owner of her grandfather's money knew the location of the wreck and was after it. Marshall had tried to force her to charter the *C. H. Marshall*, no doubt with the purpose of obtaining the loot himself. Blake grinned suddenly.

"Things don't work out so badly after all!" he thought with greater cheer than his situation warranted. "The girl herself must be on that other ship — the *John Foster!*"

Evidently the girl was known by such men as Marshall; if not personally, at least by sight. News that she was chartering a ship must have given the whole thing away, and the wolfish skipper very possibly had laid his plans to kidnap the girl that night.

Blake chuckled again, realizing that he had nipped that little game, but had been kidnapped in her stead.

"And now to see what Steelfist is going to do about it!" he concluded.

All that night he dozed fitfully. With the morning he wakened to find a blue-gray sheen against the single small porthole, low down; water was swirling against the glass and the ship was heeled over, under way again.

Four years previously, Blake had spent some months at Honolulu with his invalid father, shortly before the latter's death. Thus, when a yellow shaft of sunlight showed in the port-glass, he knew the ship was heading north, that she had passed Diamond Head, and was in harbor.

Simultaneously with the righting of the ship and the roaring clatter of the cable in her hawse-pipe, came voices overhead. Marshall was giving orders.

"Don't bother about furling sail, Mr. Forrester. Keep a short hawse — we may pull out in a hurry. I'm going to snoop around shore. No shore leave unless we have to stay overnight. In that case, let the hands take a run. I'm goin' down and interview the Dude."

A moment later Marshall's burly figure dropped into the lazarette. He planted himself before Blake, eyeing the latter coldly.

"Feel like you could be a good little man now?"

Blake, with the girl's face before his mind's eye, grinned slightly.

"I've had enough strong-arm to last me quite a while, sir," he said quietly.

Marshall eyed him in evident speculation.

"I will say you can fight like a bat out o' hell, Blake. That's why I'm here. Got use for you. What say?"

Twenty-four hours previously Blake would have set forth one and only one demand — to be set ashore, away from this hellship. Now, however, he paused reflectively. What about that girl?

"Well, sir," he returned slowly, "I don't quite understand. Are you going to put me ashore?"

To his surprise, the wolfish face darted a nod at him.

"Maybe. Don't know yet. I'm not going to leave you here when we sail, if that's what you mean. But I may have a chance to use you ashore. Feel like cuttin' up any more?"

"No," returned Blake soberly. "I've had my lesson."

Marshall rubbed his stubble of beard.

"Hm! You've signed articles, ain't you?"

"Yes, sir."

"Well, mind this: you can't get away from me, not here! Try it, and you'll wish the ropes had broke when Bower towed you overboard. I'm goin' to let you loose, an' mebbe give you a run ashore; if you try to slip away, it'll cost you skin an' —"

"I won't, sir," broke in Blake quickly. "I've signed articles and I'll stay out the cruise. You can trust my word, Captain Marshall; I'm a gentleman —"

"Not aboard this hooker, you ain't! Gentleman — huh! There's only one gent on this craft, remember that — and it's me. Now, what's caused this sudden conversion to a sense of law an' order, my bully?"

Blake caught glinting suspicion in the skipper's gaze and hastened to remove it.

"You spoke of money, didn't you? If there's a chance to see some scrapping and pull out some money, I agree to stick. Also, as I said, I've had my medicine and know when I'm down."

Marshall turned away with a nod of satisfaction. Half an hour later the Chinese steward appeared and Blake was released.

He found that the skipper had gone ashore and that Forrester had the deck. With the sole exception of Paddy Ryan the men avoided him pointedly. Like Blake himself, they were somewhat mystified by his release, but for all their hatred they feared him sufficiently to keep out of his way.

Blake's first move was to seek the forecastle. If it were true that he was to go ashore that night, here was his chance to cable home at least. He found his ten-dollar gold-piece and Forrester's revolver in the sheathing of his bunk and promptly pocketed the former. Then he lit his pipe and reflected.

"Looks as if Marshall wanted to use me," he considered. "Therefore he'll let up on me in future. Forrester's friendly, and so is Paddy Ryan. The rest are scared out. Since this ship spells deviltry for an unnamed young lady with whom I'd like to be acquainted, I guess I'll stick!"

He went on deck.

The panorama of shipping and harbor, the majestic skyline of eternal mountains behind the town, made no impression on him. He was thinking of that girl's face as he had seen it in the light from the post office doorway; and he stared moodily over the water at the square-rigged ship lying just beyond the *C. H. Marshall*.

She was the *John Foster* — slightly smaller, bluffer of bow, and not so clean of line as the *Marshall*. The two ships lay within hailing distance of each other; save for an anchor-watch, the deck of the *Foster* seemed deserted.

Toward noon, however, two things of immediate interest took place. The first came in the shape of a shore boat which drew alongside the *Foster*'s gangway; a girl stepped down the swaying ladder into the boat. Blake, sitting on the fo'c's'le head with Ryan, was galvanized into sudden interest.

The sun touched the girl's face with vivid light, bringing out each feature clear-cut as a cameo; it was The Girl beyond a doubt — the girl for whom Blake had fought on that well-remembered last night in San Francisco!

"What ye starin' at, matey?" asked Paddy Ryan. "Oh, I see — our boat's comin' out, eh? Steelfist ain't in her, though."

Blake forced his eyes away from the shore boat and turned. Sure enough, the *Marshall*'s boat was coming back, without the skipper. Bower was in her stern.

Plainly, the second mate bore important news. Long Rube came over the side like a monkey and beckoned Forrester to the rail. The two mates stood in low-voiced conversation for a brief moment, then Bower tumbled down into his boat again and pulled for shore.

To the surprise of Blake, Forrester sent a hail forward for him.

"How much fo'c's'le talk have you heard, Dude?" asked the big mate, when the two stood together at the rail. "You got some idee what we're after?"

"Some," admitted Blake, eyeing the man keenly. "Not much."

"All right. Howard's the skipper o' the *John Foster*, yonder. He's got a girl aboard. The girl is after the wreck of a ship sunk some'eres between here and Australia. Steelfist is after it too, see? But we don't know where the wreck lays, an' prob'ly the crew o' the *Foster* does — they'll know where they're bound for, anyhow."

Blake nodded quietly.

"The Ol' Man is goin' to come aboard later. Crew's goin' ashore. You an' me go ashore tonight, see? We got a scheme on what'll work. But you talk turkey right now, Dude. Do you stick with us or not? You're no liar, an' I owe you a good turn anyhow; say yes or no, and either way goes as she lays with me."

"I say yes," returned Blake, his gray eyes steady.

"Good for you, bully! Then don't go ashore with the boys, that's all."

Accordingly, when all the crew save an anchor-watch got shore-leave that afternoon, Jack Blake remained aboard. But he was less quiescent in mind than in body.

"That girl is going to have her hands full," he ruminated, kicking his heels on the fo'c's'le head and idly watching the *John Foster*. "I've constituted myself her unofficial guardian — hm! I don't know whether I'm a blame fool or a knight errant, but it looks to me as if I'd butted into a chance to be of some use in the world!"

His quiet acquiescence with Forrester's instructions — which must have come from Marshall via Long Rube — had certainly been his best plan of action. Steelfist, in the talk which had come to Blake as he lay in the lazarette, had mentioned the possibility of kidnapping the girl; Forrester had just now hinted at a scheme to get one or more of the *Foster*'s crew aboard.

Blake laughed softly to himself. "And I don't even know her name, unless it's Peabody! Well, Steelfist Marshall is going to find that I didn't sign articles to kidnap girls, anyhow! That's sure!"

What he could do was by no means clear to his mind. From all he knew, the *John Foster* had no suspicion of what the rival ship was after, and Steelfist Marshall seemed to be keeping out of sight ashore. Therefore, the girl was without warning, seemingly.

To send her a note was impossible until he could ascertain her name. Even then there were difficulties in the way. His best line of action seemed to be to get word to some one aboard the *Foster*, warn him, and then await future events. Having determined this much, Blake went below and turned in. He soon fell into a quiet sleep.

He awakened hungrily at four bells and climbed on deck to find the town and shipping twinkling with tiny lights, and the sky out past Barber's Point shot with crimson-purple in the sun's afterglow. Barely had he obtained a bite from the galley when a hail from aft apprised him that the skipper was aboard.

"Dude! Lay aft here!"

Jumping to the order, he found Marshall and Forrester by the poop ladder.

"Ain't very chummy with yourself, I s'pose?" began Marshall. "Rouse out the lamp-trimmer to keep the first anchor watch. Then you an' Mr. Forrester go ashore — that is, if you're feelin' fit and able."

There was an edge to the last sentence which caught Blake's attention.

"Quite so, sir," he replied and went forward.

So he was to be made useful, eh? Blake resolved that if it was a case of kidnapping, he would be useful in more ways than one — especially if the girl was concerned.

To his surprise, Forrester appeared a moment later with an old suit of clothes over his arm and tossed them to Blake.

"Put 'em on, Dude — you'll look better, mebbe."

"What are we going to do, sir?" asked Blake, obeying with a feeling of satisfaction.

"Have a little scrimmage, me son! You an' me an' Long Rube, an' some o' the rats. The girl I spoke of has gone to a hotel, so the *Foster*'s layin' up for a day, anyhow. We'll pick up one or two of her men an' slide out, see?"

Blake nodded.

CHAPTER VI

WITH THE HELP OF THE JAP

Half an hour later Jack Blake landed with the mate at the passenger dock. It was four years since he had been here, but the red-roofed houses, the odors of poinciana and algarroba — all seemed the same. And, with the landing, Blake quietly threw off the ship discipline and felt himself a man once more.

"I'm going to the cable office," he said calmly. "Come along, then I'm your man for the evening."

Forrester eyed him narrowly, but contented himself with a curt nod.

At the cable office Blake wrote a brief message to his long-lost friends at the Millionaires' Club and turned to the mate with a smile. But, over the smile, his gray eyes were steady. He had no intention of breaking that gold piece as yet.

"This is to inform my friends that I'm not dead," he remarked. "Thirty-five cents a word to 'Frisco — pay up!"

"Dude, you ain't lackin' in nerve!" grunted Forrester. "You're playin' square?"

"I am," returned Blake.

For an instant their eyes met. Then Forrester nodded and paid the toll.

"Now," he rejoined, as they turned away, "you an' me goes to the waterfront, Dude. Know how you come to get this chance ashore?"

"No, except that Marshall wants to make use of me. How?"

Forrester dug him in the ribs and chuckled.

"The Ol' Man wouldn't ha' missed this chance himself, not for a farm, only he hurt his iron mitt bad when you sailed into him last time. Hurt his arm, that is. Gawd knows he'll need it worser later on than he does now, too! All you got to do is to scrap as good for us as you did agin us, Dude, an' all's shipshape between us. See?"

Blake nodded, with greater inner satisfaction than he allowed to show.

"You know the *Foster* crew, then?" he asked.

"Know 'em?" grinned the mate. "You can bet we know 'em — an' they know us, more by token! When we get in port together hell pops open. The Ol' Man and Howard likes each other 'bout as much as two strange dogs."

This was not so bad, thought Blake, and for more than one reason.

Since he was evidently meant to exert himself at the side of his fo'c's'le comrades, who doubtless knew the terms of his release, here was an excellent chance to re-establish himself in their good graces.

Moreover, he was about to be given an opportunity to see for himself what manner of men were those aboard the Foster — the men entrusted with the business of that girl, whose face so persistently remained before his mind.

"What's the name of the girl you mentioned, Mr. Forrester?" he asked suddenly.

"Peabody — Mary Peabody." The mate shot him a half suspicious glance. "Mebbe you know her, huh?"

"No," laughed Blake. "I never had that pleasure."

"Huh! Well, here we are — now pay 'tention to business, Dude," came the rejoinder, as they turned toward a rambling saloon which was loud with the voices of men.

"Skippers an' mates don't come here much, but whenever the *Marshall*'s in port with the *Foster* the rule's hove overboard. Means a scrap ten times out o' ten."

The scene was new to Blake, whose previous stay in Honolulu had not gravitated him toward this locality.

From end to end of the long veranda was a reek of strong tobacco and stronger liquor. The sensuous odors of the clean night outside fled before the exhalations and uproar of seamen, who were drinking themselves happily drunk.

Blake caught sight of Ryan, Fancy Harry and a few more scattered members of the *Marshall*'s crew, then Forrester had turned him toward a far corner of the place.

Here, at one of the low tables, sat three men, who were regarded with watchful looks by the rest of the crowd. One of the three was Long Rube Bower, his pockmarked face flushed with liquor, and his eyes blazing with no love for his companions.

One of these was a red-haired, lithe, hatchet-faced seaman in heavy blue clothes, who regarded Bower with tolerant contempt; a fighting man this, and dangerous, as Blake quickly decided. Then his eyes went to the third man — and he started.

A rugged fellow, deeply tanned, who sat at the table with his huge shoulders bent forward and his two fists closed, and who was glaring steadily at Bower like a great mastiff awaiting the moment to leap — what hint of familiarity lay in that massive visage? Blake's thoughts leaped back to a fog-shrouded night — and in a flash he had it.

Here was the man whom he had seen with the girl at the Custom House on that momentous evening!

"Who's that with Bower?" he asked in a low voice, threading his way through the maze of tables beside Forrester.

"Them?" the mate chuckled. "Why, Slick Howard o' the *Foster*, o' course! That red-headed merman with him is Bingham, his mate."

Blake had no further time for reflection. Events moved fast.

As the two entered a hush had swept over the crowd; then the *Marshall*s had sent up a roar at sight of Blake following to the officers' table. Men of both parties, who had hitherto contented themselves with exchanging compliments in general, began to edge in toward the center of the room. Whatever reason Bully Forrester might have for inviting a fo'c's'le hand to drink in company with Howard and Bingham, that action could have but one result. Every man present knew it, save Blake himself, and Blake was quite conversant with the general state of affairs.

Also, he noted that the faces of Howard and Bingham were, if possible, even less conducive to confidence than those of Marshall and his officers. It was with a thrill of alarm that he faced the men to whom Mary Peabody had entrusted herself. Then they had reached the officers' table. "Take your fo'c's'le rat away from me, Forrester. He smells a little worse than you do."

Captain Howard's voice was cold and steady; he sat massively and unmoving, save that his right hand had closed on a bottle neck. The hatchet-faced mate grinned sourly and shoved back his chair. Long Rube Bower gathered his long legs beneath him and rested both hands on the table, ready to spring. Over the long, smoke-dim veranda closed down a sudden hush that was strained and tense.

"Friend o' mine, Cap'n Howard," warned Forrester slowly. "Good enough for any company I keep. Dude, what'll you have?"

For a moment Blake looked into Howard's small, slow-moving, biting eyes and realized as he did so that here was a foe worthy to meet Steelfist Marshall. Then his clean-lined features broke into a smile, and his gray eyes struck down at Howard as his quiet voice bit through the hush. "I'll take a glass of milk, thanks." The long veranda leaped into riot. As Howard flung his bottle, Bower knocked it away and flung over the table. Before the bottle struck the floor every seaman in the place was engaged, mobbing around the four smashing officers.

Blake found himself in the thick of a weaving maze of hairy fists flailing on him from every side. All his skill and agility were called into play to keep his feet as the *Foster*s rushed him; he fought away, Fancy Harry bored into the group, and the general mêlée separated into individual combats.

Finding himself left with two bull-like Sou'easters to handle, Blake managed them in a cool-headed, scientific fashion. A wild yell swept up, which told him that his shipmates had restored him to place again.

"Lookut the Dude! Wow!"

"Plaster 'em, Dude!" roared Fancy Harry, who, table-leg in hand, was mowing a swath through the hurly-burly.

Smiling, Blake put the second Sou'easter to sleep with a rocking left and whirled to give his aid to Forrester. The four officers were slugging toe to toe, however; at the same instant there pealed up a wild yell that rose shrilly over the fracas.

"Police! Clear out!"

A chair flew up and smashed the electric light cluster in a crackle of glass, and the *lanai* was plunged in darkness.

Blake felt himself borne back by the furious stampede, crashed into the flimsy rail of the veranda and went down to earth with a splintering crash. Two figures stumbled over him, and he caught a hurried word almost in his ear.

"Meet me at Waikiki — Jap place!"

It was Howard's voice, and as the figures vanished Blake caught Bingham's reply.

"Right-o! I'll be there —"

Squirming to his feet Blake dashed headlong into the shrubbery and gained the street. He had a glimpse of white-clad policemen and slipped away cautiously.

"What are Howard and Bingham doing at the Japanese Inn?" he thought, knowing the resort well. "I guess I'd better beat them to it and see what I can see. If they prove to be the right sort I'll tip 'em off about Marshall; otherwise — well, that can take care of itself."

Ten minutes later, having added shirt and collar to his rumpled attire, he boarded a Waikiki streetcar and was on the way to Diamond Head.

That brief, sharp encounter had done more than merely stimulate Jack Blake. It had showed him the all-important fact that "Slick" Howard and his mate were of much the same type as Marshall.

Not seamen of the old school, as he had hoped to find them; not bluff, honest, straight-away men who could look Marshall's kind in the eye and bid them go elsewhere; but men hard of heart, heavy of fist, who had rather spend a year after loot than a month after honest pay.

Blake's idea in seeking the Japanese Inn was quite definite. He wished to observe the skipper and mate of the *John Foster* without being seen himself, and, if possible, to make certain whether or not Mary Peabody had placed herself in unsafe hands.

He wanted very badly to glean some information which might help him to arrive at a decision regarding his own course. While cogitating how to do so, he turned in at the wooden gate of the inn and stepped up to the veranda, acutely conscious that his hand-me-downs were very different from the correct garb in which he had formerly visited this resort, four years previously.

"Misser Blek! Misser Blek!"

Blake turned, to find a grinning Jap bowing and scraping in delight. After a puzzled moment he recognized the boy as the waiter who had always served him and his father, and whom his father's tips had always brought to prompt service.

"Tani!" he exclaimed quickly. To himself he added: "I guess dad has left me a better legacy than he ever knew!"

A glance showed him that they were alone, most of the visitors being on the seaward veranda. He turned to the boy with a smile.

"Tani, you know Captain Howard?"

"I know, Misser Blek," returned Tani, his wooden features immobile again. "He come here bimeby."

"Cap'n Howard number one fella, Tani?"

The wooden face hardly showed expression — it might be said that the grain beneath showed for an instant.

"Number one fella gentleman, here. Number one fella dam pirate no here!"

Blake grinned, determined to seize this rope flung him by fate.

"I guess you've got him sized up all right, Tani. What time is he coming?"

"Him come one minute, two minute, any time coming."

"Here?"

"No *lanai* — catch room, in back-side. Have got ready."

Blake took out his gold piece and weighed it meditatively. A glitter shone in the beady eyes of Tani, who, perhaps, made a shrewd guess at what was coming.

"Tani, my father was good friend to you, eh?"

"I know, Misser Blek. What can do?"

"I want to hear what Cap'n Howard talks about. He mustn't see me. Can do?"

Tani bobbed his head.

"Can do. Come — I show you."

Blake followed the boy around through the shrubbery and they paused beneath a tree of Golden Shower, whose clusters of yellow bells brushed the side of the inn like a breath of incense. A limb of the tree ran across a cane-screened window, from which a shaded light glowed softly.

"S'pose you sit along tree. I make table by window inside. Can do?" suggested Tani hopefully. "Too much flower — no can see inside."

Blake looked up through the tree and saw that even the stars were hidden by the mass of foliage.

"Fine, Tani! Bring me a chair and some sweet syrup. Here — change this for me."

He handed Tani the gold piece and drew out his pipe. In half a moment the boy padded back with a chair, a little glass of syrup and the change. Keeping out enough to pay his way back to town, Blake returned the rest of the coins to the waiter.

"Good — run along now, and I'll not forget you next time I come."

Grinning, Tani vanished. Blake settled into his chair and filled his pipe. A sigh of satisfaction broke from him as the tobacco bit into his lungs. He was well content to have purchased this hour of peace by a few blows; afterward, he could go back to the ship and decide upon his course of action, as regarded Mary Peabody.

Like one deep note sounded the rumble of voices from the seaward veranda, drowned at moments by the slap of wavelets on the near-by beach; the laughter of women, the tinkle of glasses and the droning murmurous boom of the surf on the outer reef — these things and a thousand others formed a symphony of the tropical night.

Ten minutes passed, and Blake was beginning to wonder whether Tani might not have earned his tip by a bit of Japanese trickery — when he heard the gruff voice of Captain Howard on the veranda. There was a scrape of chairs, and then the soft voice of Tani drifted in gentle persistence.

Another scrape of chairs, grumbling voices that were silenced as screen doors closed on the speakers, and Blake heard heavy footsteps resounding in the room beside which he sat.

The screen of the window was pulled up, a match flared dimly through the leafy foliage and Blake caught the voice of Howard above him.

"Dunno's I like this stuffy inside, Bingham! Safer, though. Keep that window open so's we can hear any one snoopin' around."

"Huh!" rejoined another voice, evidently that of the mate. "You must be nervous since you shipped that skirt! Who in thunder's goin' to nose around here?"

Blake sat immobile. A door opened; there was a tinkle of glasses and the clink of money. The door closed again.

"I ain't partial to women aboard ship," said Howard, between gulps. "Dunno what she wants to come for. Won't make no differ, when all's said an' done! She won't trust me, hey?"

"No wonder," chuckled Bingham evilly, "But she stands to lose any way she plays it. She took her suitcase off to the Moana mighty quick, didn't she? S'pose she thought the atmosphere was more refined — yah! Got her orders yet?"

"That's what I come here for," grunted Howard. "Expectin' them any minute."

Blake quivered with anger.

So, then, he had been right in his suspicions! Howard was playing the very game which Marshall had mapped out for himself!

It occurred to him that his best move was to slip off to the Moana Hotel and warn Mary Peabody at once, then return to the *Marshall* and see the thing through, as he had promised. He started out of his chair, then halted abruptly.

He had best remain and find what those "orders" were, now that he was here. Also, if he were to play off Marshall against Howard, as he dimly planned, he might pick up something of service to his own skipper. A few moments would make no difference, and the Moana Hotel was not far away.

"Wish she'd ha' give me the position of her grand-daddy's mazeuma," remarked Howard irritably. "Would ha' saved a heap o' trouble. She figures we can't sail without her, 'cause she'll hang on to the dope till we get off the steamer tracks. If it wasn't for that, I'd pull out o' here. I don't feel chipper over that swine, Steelfist Marshall, hoverin' in my neighborhood."

At this Blake smiled grimly. Then the girl had not been entirely deceived after all, but was hanging on to her information! This explained a good many things.

"Huh?" queried Bingham. "Ain't the *Marshall* in on a reg'lar trip?"

"Like hell!" returned the other. "There's no such thing as a reg'lar trip with Steelfist, as you'd ought to know. Don't I see trouble every time his condemned hooker drops her mud hook alongside? He took out Sydney papers same day I cleared from 'Frisco; what's he doin' here? Bet he's the guy what tried to force Miss Peabody to charter him night afore we sailed!"

"Say, you've hit it there!" exclaimed Bingham, with a slow oath of appreciation. "But how in blazes can he know where to go if you don't know yourself?"

"He don't. But the *Marshall* can whip the sheets off the *Foster* when it comes to sailing, see? We can't stop him pullin' out after us, can we? Not that I give two darns for him and his iron mitt! When we drop anchor over that hulk, I'll have the coin out of her in spite of the skirt, Steelfist Charley Marshall, or the devil himself! Only we could ha' done without the extra trouble."

The two fell silent.

Jack Blake began to regret having so easily passed his word to Marshall and to Forrester. It began to look very much as though Mary Peabody, alone on the *Foster*, would have stern need of a friend; could he have left Marshall here and shipped with Howard, he might yet be of some service.

On the other hand, after getting his warning, the girl might charter another ship altogether, and he was bound by his word to finish the voyage on the *Marshall*.

"I'll wait for those orders," he told himself, "then I'll hit for the Moana Hotel, tell her what's up, and go find Forrester. That —"

He paused, as a knock sounded from the room above.

"Who's that?" growled Howard.

"Me, Tani. Got message from Miss Peabody. Boy bring him."

The door was opened and closed. After a short interval of silence there was a crash as Howard brought down his fist on the table.

"What d'ye know about this, Bingham! She's gone aboard already; says she wants to sail by midnight! Bet she got a sight o' Steelfist somewheres an' recognized him —"

But Blake heard no more. Slipping from his chair he was already striding toward the entrance of the grounds, with blank dismay in his heart. Mary Peabody would never get that warning now!

CHAPTER VII
THE FINN AND THE SUITCASE

As his car sped toward town Blake's lips clenched in grim resolve.

"Missed my chance," he thought bitterly. "I daren't send a note aboard the *Foster* — she'd never get it in the world! No, I've got to get hold of Forrester and the men, then let Marshall know that Howard is going to sail at midnight. If I advance Marshall's game, I advance my own. Then — my time will come later."

Since Marshall had expected to remain till next day with the *John Foster*, Blake knew that he would find the mates and the crew still ashore. So, leaving the car at the edge of town, he located a boat-boy on the waterfront who gave him the names of some houses of call for officers.

Blake started on his rounds hastily, for it was now drawing on toward midnight.

"There's good in all evil, just the same," he consoled himself. "My alacrity in this matter will convince Steelfist that I'm playing square with him. And at the finish — by thunder, I'll find some way to counter him and Howard together!"

At his second stopping place he obtained news of the two mates. Five minutes later he ran them to earth in a private room of a saloon.

"Hello, Dude!" exclaimed Forrester. "Thought you had been put away. You can cert'nly scrap — eh, Rube?"

Long Rube condescended to lend a word of assent. Both men were plain blue water ruffians when it came to handling a crew; and, to a great extent, they had to be such. Yet neither of them was the man to withhold appreciation, ashore, of the qualities which at sea made Blake dangerous to them.

"Did you get any of them?" asked Blake quietly.

"Nary one — the police broke in too quick."

"I suppose you know that the *Foster* sails at midnight?"

The two men stared at him in startled surmise. Having nothing to conceal in the story, Blake told exactly what he had overheard at the Japanese inn.

At the first words Bower would have dashed off to round up the men, but Forrester held him back, bidding Blake give the whole yarn.

"Lord!" broke out the angry second mate. "We been sittin' here gammin' while Howard's heavin' short —"

"Run along, then," commanded Forrester with an oath. "Round up the crowd, an' get busy."

Bower disappeared on the run. The mate, more leisurely, started toward the landing-place with Blake.

"We can sail rings around the *Foster*," said Forrester slowly. "But when the Ol' Man saw the girl take her gear ashore to the hotel he nat'rally thought the Foster was good for a couple o' days anyhow. So the crew's ashore an' hell's to pay. Are any of the Foster's crew ashore?"

"Very likely," nodded Blake. "Howard only got his sailing orders when I was there, a half-hour ago. It —"

"Then meet me at the landin' stage — keep under cover — I'll be back —"

Whirling abruptly, Forrester departed at a lumbering run, leaving Blake to continue by himself. Once at the landing-place Blake settled down with his pipe in the shadow of some piled kegs, where he could keep a watch on all things.

The place seemed absolutely deserted, however. Five minutes later a number of native boatmen appeared hastily; urging them on was Forrester, who left them and came over to join Blake, puffing and dripping with sweat.

"Holy Gawd, if it works!" he panted.

"What?" asked Blake nonchalantly.

"Wait an' see. I — listen to that! Listen to that! Ain't it hell? There's Howard gettin' his hook, blast him! Ain't none of his cursed crowd ashore?"

Out from the harbor the metallic clank of windlass pawls shattered the night, and sharp commands snapped out from the darkness. The mate cursed fluently.

The sounds ceased, however, and as the riding lights of the two ships remained steady, Forrester's curses ceased also.

Howard's ship was evidently waiting for something or somebody. When her anchor was broken out her riding light would come down, and sidelights would show in her fore rigging. So her crew must still be ashore, in part.

"Marshall ahoy!" rang out a thick voice near the kegs. "Vot vas —"

"Rube's gettin' 'em," snapped the mate, leaping up.

A dark figure stumbled down toward the water and disclosed itself as that same Dutchman who had been hung by the thumbs to the sheerpole one morning for commiserating Blake's tortures.

The Dutchman was drunk, and Forrester ran him to a waiting native, who tossed him aboard and set out for the ships. Barely had the mate rejoined Blake, when a second figure appeared, with a grunting hail.

"Yon Foster! Hey, Yon Foster boat!"

Without a word Forrester leaped forward, caught the speaker, and swung him toward the light of the dock lamps. Then even Jack Blake allowed a grin to escape him.

The man carried a small leather suitcase. He was dressed as only a Finn foremast hand knows how to dress for shore leave — hard felt hat, gray-and-red neck muffler, and shrieking hand-me-down suit, pressed by rolling into a ball and jamming into a tarpaulin bag. He teetered on high-heeled shoes that would have taxed the ability of a cowboy to the limit.

"Hey, you!" demanded Forrester roughly. "Where ye bound? What ye doin' with that suitcase?"

"I bring from Waikiki, sir," stammered the Finn, nervously. "I tek to Miss Pebbody in Yon Foster — she give me big call down for come late. I go 'board —"

"Gawd's own luck!" breathed the mate, hoarsely.

Like a cat he flung himself bodily upon the seaman. The Finn had taken warning and ducked away; only to trip over his high heels, however, and the next instant Forrester was on him.

"Ow!"

The agonized cry broke from the Finn as the mate's heavy boot landed in his ribs. He crashed headlong to the planking. There came a thud of boots stumbling down the wharf, and Forrester whirled on Blake with a sudden snarl.

"What you standin' there for like a fool spike? Don't stare questions — jump! Get them men into the boats, you idiot!"

Blake obeyed. He realized instantly that this Finn, having been sent to the hotel for the girl's suitcase, must be a man to be trusted, either by Howard or by the girl herself. Therefore he would be a good source of information.

Three men appeared, dazed with drink, and Blake ran them down to the waiting native boats. Then came Paddy Ryan, and after him Long Rube Bower, cursing like a fiend.

"Ain't another man in sight," he cried profanely. "The rest must ha' gone up to the Punch Bowl an' fallen in —"

"Cutlip Sullivan and young Boston went up to Mongovan's place, sir," spoke up Paddy Ryan. "Big Frank Keough's drunk in that bar by the Institute —"

"Go get 'em," blazed out Forrester, turning savagely on the second mate. "An' stay till ye do get 'em, see? Come on, Dude — pile in!"

Blake jumped into the boat with Paddy Ryan, the mate, and the senseless Finn, and they were rowed out to the ship. On the way, they passed the *Foster*, and in a whisper Forrester explained his strategy.

"I got them native boys to bring out everybody to the *Marshall* — see? If any o' the *Foster*'s crowd is ashore, they come to us."

"They're probably all aboard," returned Blake. "Howard must have been waiting for this Finn."

"He'll wait till hell freezes over then!"

They found Steelfist Charley stalking the deck in fuming rage. To avoid the imminent outburst of wrath, Bully Forrester promptly brought forward his prisoner and explained what had taken place.

Meantime, Blake secured the girl's suitcase and smuggled it into the fo'c's'le. To think of that suitcase being pawed over by Marshall and

Forrester revolted him. Besides, it might contain private information which would be of service to him.

"Guess I'm some angel guardian, eh," he thought with a chuckle.

He dropped the suitcase into the chain locker where he, as ordinary seaman, would be the first man sent when getting up anchor. Then he returned on deck to find a different atmosphere.

Steelfist seemed to have sloughed his rage. His grim face was a mesh of grinning wrinkles, and he glared over the rail at the *Foster*'s riding light as if enjoying the impatience that must be consuming the rival skipper at the non-arrival of the Finn.

Almost together, eight bells clanged out from the two ships. But still the *John Foster* floated idly, her topsails hanging in the buntlines, and her jib boom a raffle of loosed headsails. From the *Marshall* Blake could make out the glimmer of Bingham's lantern on the fo'c's'lehead, and as her riding light swung to her heave it cast vagrant gleams on the men at the windlass brakes.

One bell, and two bells, and a shore boat pulled alongside with more of the *Marshall*'s errant crew. Still the *Foster* swung to her shortened cable, and Steelfist chuckled more audibly at each passing moment.

Boat after boat sheered alongside, until all the crew but Cutlip Sullivan, young Boston, and Big Frank Keough were accounted for. Long Rube was working hard, and as the *Foster* showed no signs of life Marshall sent the men below to sleep or to stand by for an early call.

Blake went with the rest, certain now that Howard would not slip away from Steelfist Marshall that night at least. He had just got asleep when he was roused up by a sharp dig in the ribs.

"Hey, Dude! Wake up, you grampus — this is the mate talkin' to you!"

"Eh? Yes, sir!" Blake swung up at once.

"Where's that suitcase the Finn had?"

Blake stared sleepily, with an excellent air of surprise. The dim fo'c's'le resounded with full-bodied snores.

"The Finn had it, sir," he replied. "He must have dropped it when you piled on him."

"You fat-headed sojer, o' course he did!" Forrester heaved up with an air of disgust. "If he don't say nothin' about it, you needn't, see? The Ol' Man would be sore as blazes — no use goin' back to look for it now."

"All right, sir," responded Blake and rolled over to sleep with an inward chuckle.

At five in the morning the hands were turned out, and the usual ship's business was put in progress. Opposite, the *John Foster* swung to her anchor still. Blake found that the three seamen were still missing, and so was Long Rube Bower.

Steelfist had not yet appealed on deck, but at six o'clock the mate came forward after getting his coffee and opened the sail room where the hapless Finn had been confined during the night.

Blake was plying the squeegee when Forrester passed and felt a wave of loathing as the mate flung him a grin of cold cruelty.

"The Finn's goin' to talk now," said Forrester, leering. "Steelfist's got somethin' aft that'll cure his dumbness!"

"You won't get much out of him, sir," returned Blake. "What there was to know was probably in that suitcase. You don't suppose the Dutchman knows anything about it?" he added, suddenly.

The mate paused at the locker door.

"Gripes, yes!" he exclaimed. "I'll go see that big Dutchman."

He walked back along the waist to where the Dutchman was working. Blake swiftly slipped to the door of the locker.

"Hey, you Finn!" he said quickly. "If you can stick it out, don't tell them anything! I've got the suitcase safe — I'm Miss Peabody's friend, savvy?"

The Finn stared wildly at him. He was lashed fast on top of a pile of sails, and his eyes were red with lack of sleep. He seemed to take heart at Blake's words.

"Tank ju," he muttered. "It don't mek no differ. If Miss Pebbody know I not come, she can sail quick."

"I'll attend to that."

Blake nodded, one eye on the mate. He resumed his work, speaking over his shoulder the while.

"When you cross the poop I'll hail the *Foster*. You throw up your arms or make a stir — they'll see you. Maybe Steelfist will forget you in his hurry to follow. Savvy that?"

"Ya," returned the Finn.

Blake, satisfied that he had set matters going well, walked away to put up his squeegee as the mate returned with a shake of the head.

Forrester marched the luckless Finn aft, having unbound him. Blake hurried from the bo'sun's locker and followed, while the rest of the crew gathered to watch proceedings.

As the captive reached the poop, Blake let out a laughing hail.

"What's the matter, *John Foster*? Afraid to hoist anchor for fear you'll catch the gale that blew away last week?"

The remark served its purpose of attracting attention. As Forrester turned with an oath and a snarl to "Shut up!" the Finn flung out his arms.

Instantly a shout arose from the *John Foster* that startled the seabirds into flight — a shout of rage and vengeance. Before that shout died away the *Foster*'s topsail-yards were jerked aloft to an improvised chanty which evoked a howl of rage from the *Marshall*.

> "Oh, Steelfist's dead an' gone below —
> Oh, we say so — an' we hopes so;

Oh, Steelfist's dead an' he'll go below;
Oh, poor — ol' — man!

"He's deader'n the bolt on the fo'c'sle door —
Oh, we say so — an' we hopes so;
Oh, he'll never knock us dead no more —
Oh, poor — ol' — man!"

The *John Foster* was off.

CHAPTER VIII

FACING A CRISIS

Roused by the shouts, Steelfist Marshall was on deck in two jumps.

He took in the position at once when the clank-clank rattled from the *Foster*'s windlass, and her foreyards were braced aback to pay her off as the anchor broke out.

"What's started the blame fool off?" he cried furiously. Then, catching sight of Forrester at the rail, "Man the windlass, you pop-eyed owl! Call all hands! Where's Bower?"

Forrester was taken aback. He stared at the *Foster* with mouth agape, then his eyes went to the Finn and back to Blake, as if to piece together the parts of a puzzle.

"What're you staring at, you dumb image?" roared the furious skipper. "Where's Bower? Wake up!"

"He went ashore at daylight," growled Forrester. "Them three men ain't showed up yet."

At this, Marshall broke into a storm of curses. Now a shout from the *Foster* announced the breaking-out of the anchor, and her head paid off under the thrust of her backed foreyards.

A man ran aloft on each mast to loose the top-gallant sails, and her foreyards came around handily to a runaway chorus, every line of which reached the ears of the raging Marshall as the *Foster* gathered way and stood across his stern.

> *"Oh, what shall he do with his drunken sailors.*
> *What shall he do with his drunken sailors,*
> *What shall he do with his drunken sailors,*
> *Early in the morning!*
> *"Way, hay, there she rises —*
> *Way, hay, there she rises!*
> *Hay! Whoop! There she rises,*
> *Early in the morning!"*

Sail after sail was sheeted home aboard the *John Foster*, and the liquid music of her bow wave burbled along her black sides as she rapidly drew nearer, leaning gracefully to the fresh air of the morning.

At her weather rail stood Captain Howard, bull-like and massive, his red features alight with leering triumph. He leaned out, holding on by the mizzen-royal backstay, and directed a hail at the *Marshall*:

"Stung, ain't you?" he barked, his deep voice ringing clear. "The Finn ain't no consequence, long's we know where he is. Take him an' welcome! So long, Cap'n Marshall! Hope your long an' useless greaser finds them drunken sailors for you afore night!"

Marshall leaped to the rail with a curse and shook his steel fist at the passing ship.

"You keep away and crack on, blast you!" he roared. "I'll find what I want from the Finn, and I'll beat your bloody ol' hooker yet!"

"Finn don't know anything," came the derisive answer, as the *John Foster* pointed up for the reef entrance.

At this instant a shout rang down from aloft. Paddy Ryan had been working on a broken ratline halfway up the main rigging. The *Foster* had run so close that he could get a clear view of her decks.

"Hey, Cap'n Marshall!" he shouted down, flinging out an arm toward the other ship. "Git yer glasses! See if that ain't Cutlip Sullivan roped up in the waist of her!"

Marshall leaped for the mizzen-rigging, glasses in hand, and Blake lost no time in jumping with the rest for a view. The *Foster* showed her stern, and the men were all but hidden, but a roar of rage broke from the *Marshall*.

Steelfist slid down the topmast backstay and turned on the mate.

"Who's missing, Forrester? They got three men roped up, there!"

"Young Boston, Keough, an' Sullivan, sir," returned the mate quickly.

"Where in perdition is that long crab of a Bower?" broke out the wrathful skipper. "Bo'sun! You go get him — and by the Lord, if you liquor up I'll flay you! Slip ashore an' hustle him. Tell him if he ain't aboard in half an hour I'll break him an' put him to work in the galley! If you come back without him, I'll flake you!"

Fancy Harry beckoned one of the passing native boats and was gone.

"Man that windlass!" bawled Steelfist, in a fury. "Loose them tops'ls!"

As the men leaped about their work, Marshall eyed the Finn, who stood where Forrester had left him. The fellow looked grotesque in his sadly battered finery, and his pale, watery blue eyes blinked fearfully at the skipper.

"What's your name?" whipped out Marshall suddenly.

"Ole Kafban, sir."

"Mr. Forrester! Pass me some small line!"

As he took the line, Steelfist cast one eye at the rigging, then seemed to alter his intention. Striding to the shrinking figure of Ole Kafban, he merely tied one end of the line to one wrist, taking a turn around his own left hand with the other end. Thus he held the Finn at the end of a fathom of tether, like a dog on the leash.

"Ole Kafban, did you know my three men had been carried aboard the *Foster*?" he demanded, fastening his glittering eyes on the seaman.

"Naw, sir —"

The line tightened, and Ole flung up his free arm in terror.

"Naw, sir! I vas 'shore all day. Dond't — Dond't!"

"Don't get scared, son," Marshall laughed grimly. "My men all love me, I'm so gentle!"

He twisted another turn of the line about his wrist, drawing the Finn a foot closer to him.

"I don't believe you did know about those men, Ole." Marshall's face held the wolfish look that augured an outburst of passion. "But you can tell where the *Foster*'s bound for, can't you now?"

The line tightened, almost imperceptibly.

"Ay dond't knaw, sir, Ay dond't knaw! Capen Howard dond't knaw himself — oh, Fader!"

Marshall suddenly jerked on the line.

The Finn lurched toward him, stumbling, and the steel fist crunched viciously into the side of the helpless man. With a low groan, Ole Kafban slid to his knees and went down in a limp heap, fainting more from terror than from the sickening blow.

What else the skipper had in store for the Finn was postponed by the arrival of Fancy Harry Lovell and the second mate.

"Dump this rat into the fo'c's'le, Mr. Forrester," snapped Marshall. "He'll sign on when we're away, or we'll waste a length of canvas on him. Are you hove short?"

"Cable's 'most up an' down, sir. Break out in two minutes."

The senseless Finn was dropped into the fo'c's'le. As Bower came over the side, he sought refuge from the skipper's evident wrath in his duties and took his station for getting under way. The *John Foster*, heeling to the strong trade wind, was like a fairy toy in the distance.

"Heave away for'ard!" sang out Marshall, his eye on the diminishing speck.

"Heave away," echoed Forrester, and the men walked the capstan around in silence, save for the jar and surge of the cable links.

"Anchor's apeak, sir!" cried the mate.

"Up with the tops'ls," came the curt order. "All three together, now! Lively men, lively!"

Divided into three groups, with the mates, the cook, and even the Chinese steward lending a hand, the men at the halyards sorely missed the beef of the three absent men.

The foretopsail was mastheaded first. While the hands ran to give a pull on the main, Forrester directed Blake to bring the Finn from the fo'c's'le. Blake slipped down to find Ole Kafban sitting on the floor, shivering in fear.

"We're short-handed, Ole. Slip up and bear a hand, and maybe Steelfist will go light on you. We're after the *Foster*. Remember now, I'm your friend and the friend of Miss Peabody. Chase along with you!"

Somewhat reassured, Ole lumbered up the ladder. Blake, remembering that he had not been sent to stow chain, darted to the chain locker hatch.

He found the chain below piled in lumps, just as it had fallen from the windlass, and it was plain that no one had been spared from the capstan bars to stow it. Therefore, the suitcase was safe for the time, buried under a ton of chain.

Jumping for the deck again, Blake joined the Finn and they both tailed on to the lee fore-brace as the ship canted away on the port tack and started her stern chase.

Once outside the harbor the *C. H. Marshall* was not slow to feel the hurl of the brisk quartering wind that whistled and twanged in her taut rigging. As by degrees she felt the added impulse of royals and topgallant sails, it became evident that she was holding the *Foster*, and Steelfist Marshall grew into calmer mood.

While they worked together, Blake made shift to tell the Finn about the situation in which Mary Peabody had got herself. Ole's pale blue eyes lighted with a dog-like affection at the girl's name, and Blake understood that the man's simple soul was wholly devoted.

"You be good feller," said the Finn, looking hard into Blake's steady eyes. "S'pose mabbe Capen Marshall hit me some more?"

"If he does, I'll do my best for you, Ole. But there's no harm in telling all you know, because the only way in which we can help Miss Peabody is to reach the position of the wreck ourselves. Unless we do so, Howard will have the game all to himself," said Blake.

For a moment Ole studied over this statement, then nodded solemnly.

"Sure. You be good feller. Right! Ay knaw yoost so much — Miss Pebbody say to sail nine hoonderd mile sout'. After dat, she give position. Capen Howard don't knaw no more."

Cogitating over this information, Blake determined to take it aft at once. Such procedure might save the Finn future torture and would certainly better his own standing with the skipper. Blake knew well enough that his only means of helping Mary Peabody lay in gaining the confidence of Steelfist Marshall.

Accordingly, Blake took himself aft and saluted the scowling skipper cheerfully. Steelfist was already conversant with all that had taken place ashore.

"Cap'n Marshall, I've been talking to that Finn and I find that he knows as much as Cap'n Howard himself. The *John Foster* is to sail nine hundred miles south, to get out of steamer lanes; then Miss Peabody gives the actual position of the wreck and the —"

"Dude, look out how you try your funny wheezes on me!" broke in Steelfist, his black curls dancing in the wind. "Why in thunder did he tell you this? He wouldn't tell me a blasted word."

Blake smiled evenly. His gray eyes were cold and held Steelfist Marshall's gaze intently.

"Your methods were somewhat — er — terrifying, sir," he said quietly. "I simply asked him, and he told me. You seemed to have scared him to death."

"Hm!" grunted the other. "Think he's on the level, do you? If he's lying he'll make shark bait!"

"Yes, I believe him, sir. If I may make a suggestion, he wouldn't be a bad one to sign on in place of Sullivan. He's a good seaman and might help us a lot."

Marshall's glittering eyes studied Blake's clean, hard face for a moment.

"I like bullies o' your sort, Dude," he replied unexpectedly. "You've done some good work for us, and I'm glad you've found your senses. Send the Finn aft. I'll sign him on and hold you responsible for his conduct. How's that?"

"Fine, sir," nodded Blake. "He seems to like me, and I'll agree to manage him."

So Ole Kafban went aft and was duly signed on, and Jack Blake considered that he had done a good day's work for himself and Mary Peabody.

His position had been secured, so far as the officers were concerned. With his shipmates, also, the fracas at Honolulu had helped him; he was no longer avoided and seemed to have regained his old standing to some extent. Paddy Ryan had been shifted into the other watch, so that Blake saw little of him now.

Before the sun lipped the western sea-line that evening the *C. H. Marshall* had drawn up on the *Foster* sufficiently to prove her superior speed, and Steelfist's scowl had been left behind with the wake.

That Howard was uncomfortable was plainly evident. Every device to pinch speed out of his ship, even to the rigging of makeshift studdingsails, was tried; but the *Marshall* under plain sail easily held her place, and Steelfist smiled in contempt when his rival's makeshifts were taken in for the night.

Through the night continued the chase, an arc light of a moon pouring its brilliance over the deep-breathing ocean and limning the *John Foster* in shining patches of radiant silver.

Toward morning, however, the moon failed. The three hours before dawning were black as Erebus, and when at last the blazing sun cupped over the horizon to announce another day, the sea was bare as a desert. The *John Foster* had vanished.

Long Rube Bower had the watch. The moment he satisfied himself that he had not lost his eyesight, that the *Foster* was actually gone, he dived below and aroused Steelfist Marshall.

The skipper was on deck in his pajamas, sweeping the sea with his binoculars before Forrester's bulk loomed in the companionway. Nothing was in sight. Steelfist sprang to the mizzen-royal-yard, swept the horizon vainly, then slid down the backstay with a sounding curse.

"Get that Finn!" he snarled, his face suffused with evil blood. At his tone the business of washing decks was suspended promptly.

Ole was below, and Blake dropped his broom and slid down to forestall Long Rube, heartsick at thought of the simple Finn. He gripped Ole and had the man awake instantly.

"Wake up — they're coming for you! Do you know anything more about the *Foster*'s port? Tell me sharp, now!"

"Ay toldt ju ever't'ing Ay knaw," asserted Ole, panic in his pale eyes.

"Is there anything in the suitcase?" persisted Blake, hearing the steps of Bower at the hatch.

"Mabbe — mabbe — Ay dond't t'ink so," whimpered the Finn.

Blake dived forward into the recess of the ship's eyes, as Bower came down and hurled himself on Ole. When the Finn had been dragged bodily upward, Blake cautiously lifted the cabin-locker hatch and dropped to the cables below.

"If I don't find something to save that fellow, Steelfist will murder him!" he thought, grim-lipped.

Working feverishly, yet with a modicum of noise, he tore aside tier after tier of the heavy chain until he came to a crushed, shapeless brown mass which had once been a suitcase. The lock had survived, but the case itself had been burst apart in every seam.

A shriek of agony pealed along the deck above, echoing under the straining foresail and carrying with startling clarity to Blake. Desperately he tossed up the mass of things to the fo'c's'le above, got them into his bunk, and searched for he knew not what.

Then he felt a sudden thrill — amid the soft garments, whose touch brought a tinge of red to his cheeks, he found a notebook.

Another scream rang out. Blake ran to the hatch and turned over the pages of the notebook.

They seemed blank; then, written in pencil at the back of the cover, he found what he wanted. "Southwest by south, 650 miles."

The scrawl meant nothing clear to him, yet he felt that here lay the clue to the whole thing. At the same time, it was nothing that he could use to save Ole. The few words told him nothing.

Were the fact known that he had hidden the suitcase, his own fate would be swift and bitter. He caught up his hidden revolver and pocketed it.

Another and prolonged scream from the after deck sent him to his bunk again. Hurriedly heaping the scattered garments to one end, he threw his other things over them in effectual concealment. Then he jumped to the ladder.

"I'll have to face him down," he muttered, "anger-muscles" playing in his cheeks as his jaw clenched! "The low-lived murderers! I'm getting tired of knuckling under to a set of roughnecks! By the Lord, I'll face Marshall down, and if there's any scrapping done, I'll shoot him and take command of the cursed ship myself!"

All of which held more raving than sense. But, as Blake swung up to the deck and glanced aft, a slow curse of fervid loathing broke from him at sight of the scene being enacted on the poop.

Then he started aft, hand on his revolver.

CHAPTER IX

TAKING BIG CHANCES

All hands stood watching the poop, with frightened, angry faces; Fancy Harry Lovell was cursing in a low voice. Even the hardened mates were not grinning as they usually did, at the skipper's pleasantries.

In the weather mizzen rigging hung Ole Kafban, spread-eagled. His wrists were lashed, one to the forward, one to the after shrouds; his ankles, stretched wide apart, were lashed fast to the hauling-part of the weather main brace, where it led inboard. He was stripped to the waist.

Around his hanging, agonized figure stepped Steelfist Marshall, his terrible right arm poised, coolly picking the spots where he could inflict the greatest agony with the least chance of rendering his victim insensible.

The Finn's back and sides were streaked with livid weals and purple bruises, and blood was trickling over his skin. The skipper was speaking to him in a voice repellent in its icy ferocity; the Finn's groans were mingled with moaned denials and abject pleas for mercy.

Blake's absence from the deck had passed unnoted. His gray eyes like ice, he now walked up to the skipper; his even, passionless voice seemed to bite into Marshall as he spoke.

"Captain Marshall, this man has told you all he knows. You'll beat no more out of him."

Marshall turned to him with an oath and drew back his right arm. But Blake's steady eyes and unmirthful smile halted him.

"Better not try it, sir," went on the American, hearing a mutter of applause from the crew behind him, "unless you want to be jumped. The men won't stand this kind of thing — and neither will I. Leave that Finn alone. I guaranteed his good faith, and I repeat it."

"Huh?" growled Marshall venomously. "What you know 'bout him?"

"No more than you. Mind, I told you that I'd stick, and so I will; so will the men. But we won't stick for this kind of business, cap'n. The *Foster*'s course was simply altered to fool you."

Perhaps Marshall noted that Blake's hand was resting in his jacket-pocket. His scowling glance went to the mates, then swept over the sullen faces of the men at the foot of the ladder.

"Take the rat for'ard," he growled, staring down the men one by one and then fetching his eyes to Blake. "You, Dude — what you grinnin' about?"

"I'd like to have a word with you in private, sir," smiled Blake.

Marshall eyed him half suspiciously.

"Come aft in an hour. I want to get dressed an' have a cup o' coffee 'thout any stinkin' fo'c's'le rats around."

Having thus saved his blusterous dignity, Steelfist tramped below.

In the fo'c's'le Blake ministered to the luckless Finn's bruises in a way that brought the dog-like expression back into Ole's watery eyes. The rest of the watch were rousing out for breakfast and had no time or breath to waste, so that Ole and Blake were left severely alone.

When the frightened, hysterical man was quieted down Blake sat talking with him for a little. He questioned Ole about the notebook and directions, but found that the Finn knew absolutely nothing.

The man's affection for Mary Peabody was self-evident, however. The girl had saved him from some manner of brutality aboard the *Foster*, and Ole spoke of her with tears in his watery blue eyes.

At eight bells Blake went on deck. The morning was perfect. Tiny whitecaps played at the summits of the long, even swells; a graceful roll of foamy sea curled away from the sharp stem of the ship; from horizon to zenith the blazing blue sky was flecked with woolly puffs of cloud hurrying athwart the ship's course.

Every yard of canvas bellied full from yards and stays, snoring with a deep thrum under the wind, thrusting the *C. H. Marshall* fair on her southerly course. Blake was not long in getting a bluff hail from Forrester, telling him that the Old Man wanted him in the cabin.

He found Marshall sitting at his table, the Chinaman hovering near.

"Captain Marshall," said Blake quietly, having long since decided on the story to be told, "you may remember that I was at Waikiki just before we sailed, and I heard Captain Howard and Bingham talking over their plans?"

"Bully Forrester told me all that," grunted the skipper. "What's up?"

"I'm not sure myself, sir," smiled Blake. "But here are some figures which may mean something to you: 650 miles, south-west by south. They may, of course, mean nothing; I'm sorry I didn't speak of them before, however."

Marshall frowned and sat for a moment in silence. Then, gruffly bidding the steward leave the cabin, he went to a locker and unrolled a large chart on the table.

"Huh!" he remarked. "Nothin' on the chart there, Dude. Leastways not that course an' distance from Honolulu. Sure you ain't forgot nothin' more?"

"That's all I know," nodded Blake, with a swift sense of disappointment.

After all, there had been nothing to indicate that the pencil-scrawl referred to the great secret. He had possibly jumped at conclusions in a most unwarranted manner —

"Hold on!" broke out the skipper, with an oath. "Nine hundred south —"

Bending over the chart once more, Marshall caught up a pencil and scribbled down a calculation. He verified it, then flung down the pencil with an exclamation of amazed delight.

"By Jupiter! Shouldn't wonder if you've hit it after all, Dude! Here's the point nine hundred miles south o' Honolulu — see? Figuring your six-fifty sou'-west by south, we'd fetch Fulai!"

Blake thrilled to the words. The skipper worked another brief calculation and leaped up.

"Dude, we'll take the chance! The course from here is sou'-sou'-west, 'bout twelve hundred mile. If it's the right dope, and it certainly looks it, then by glory we'll lick the stern off that blasted Howard by a week!"

Marshall sprang on deck and gave out the new course. Blake went forward again, and in an hour every man aboard was conversant with the news. Only then did Jack Blake fully realize that he had not only Steelfist Marshall to cope with, but Marshall's crew as well.

From the skipper down to the steward, every man aboard was filled with thoughts of loot. Each watch yarned of treasure-trove and "easy money"; Fancy Harry and the rest of the older hands told of Bully Hayes and other famous characters by the hour. The only foremast hand who went about his work and said nothing was Ole Kafban.

Blake had cherished hopes of appealing to Paddy Ryan's better nature and Celtic chivalry, but soon saw that the little Irishman was as mad as the rest about the object of the cruise. Reluctantly, Blake drew aside and stood alone, with the Finn for a weak anchor; he was none so certain of his own status that he dared endanger the position which he had gained.

Steelfist Marshall was taking a long chance on heading for Fulai — a small coral island well off the steam routes. If all went well, they would reach the island in less than a week. Whether or not this was the spot for which the *John Foster* was aiming was another question.

From the Finn Blake learned that the state of affairs aboard the *Foster* was much the same as on the *Marshall* — officers and crew bent on the one object of getting the treasure. That Mary Peabody was in any present danger was most unlikely. The exact location of the wreck was probably her own secret and would be so until the island was reached.

After that, thought Blake grimly, the event would lie largely with himself and with the finger of Fate.

The days flew swiftly, while the *C. H. Marshall* boomed along steadily under the trades. Then, on the sixth morning, all lingering doubt and anxiety was settled when the lookout aloft reported the patched topgallant-sail of the *John Foster* in sight abeam, on a course convergent with that of the *Marshall*.

For the first time in days, Steelfist's rugged face gleamed in a smile void of ferocity. He urged the utmost from his ship and by nightfall he was close up with, and to windward of, the *John Foster*.

Howard, too, was driving for all he was worth; it must have become apparent that the *C. H. Marshall* was bound straight for the same port, and that she had the heels of him.

All through the night the *Marshall* edged down on the *Foster*. Toward dawn the two ships were within hailing distance, and through megaphones of canvas there began an exchange of sarcasm, compliment and personality which made Blake trust that Mary Peabody was keeping well out of ear-shot.

All hands were on deck, hanging to the rail and enjoying the exchange between Howard and Steelfist; and, every sail drawing a rapful, the *Marshall* slowly forged ahead of her rival.

Then came a sudden yell from Forrester, in the bows.

"Look out! By Gawd, she's tackin' into us!"

No one had noticed how perilously close the two ships were; and, with his extra large crew, Captain Howard tacked his ship like a schooner. When Forrester's yell pealed up, she was gathering way and bearing down with a smother of bow wave, aiming fair at the bows of the *Marshall*.

"Weather braces! Right yer hellum, ye fool!"

Steelfist followed his deep shout by leaping himself to the lee cro'-jack brace. His action blanched the faces of the oldest seaman aboard, and even Blake understood the desperate chance being taken.

With the *Foster* foaming nearer, an ominous shape spitting forth jeering yells and curses, the *Marshall*'s yards were swung until she was caught flat aback. Every sail thundered back on the masts, and the whole ship groaned with the tremendous strain of it.

For sixty tense seconds Jack Blake held his breath, gazing fearfully aloft, praying that the gear would hold. The odds were even that the masts would be wrenched out of her, that she would go under stern first, or that she would hold.

But Steelfist knew his ship, and his judgment proved sound. The ship staggered, stopped and then slowly forged astern. The *John Foster* shot across her bows so close that a man might have leaped from ship to ship.

That was "Slick" Howard's last chance, for the *Marshall* gathered way again before he could think of tacking, and in half an hour was far beyond his reach. Yet this had been enough to show Jack Blake that he was playing a game with desperate men, with Hatred sitting at each elbow, and human life flung into the discard.

"By the Lord," he thought, gazing after the dim splotch of the *Foster*'s canvas, "this is a man's play! And when I sit into the game I'll play it like a man — for the sake of the little girl over yonder!"

At daybreak came the end of the first round, when a blue mass ahead resolved itself into an island, tiny, reef-encircled, yet slumbrously beautiful — a verdure-clad hump jutting from the sea — Fulai.

Steelfist himself mounted to the foreyard to scan the reef for an opening, with the *John Foster* converging on the island abeam. The entrance appeared, and although the *Foster* held on past it Steelfist kept to his course, shouting profanely that he had been fooled enough by "Slick" Howard. He shortened sail, none the less.

Too late the skipper saw the Foster shoot through the reef a mile farther on and slide into the glassy calmness of a lagoon. A moment later Steelfist let out a deep shout and came sliding to the deck.

"Wear, Forrester, wear!" he roared frantically.

Braces were hastily manned; the mizzen staysails rattled down, and the outer and flying jibs that had been taken in were sent flying up the stays again.

The ship's head paid off, away from the half-visible froth of surf under her forefoot, but it was too late. A tremulous shudder ran through the vessel; there came a gentle grating, and the *C. H. Marshall* quietly rested on a hidden spur of reef.

"Fooled again, by Heaven!" quoth Forrester.

CHAPTER X

PREPARING FOR CRIME

Steelfist Marshall was far too wise an old seadog to abandon the chase merely because his keel was wedged between two fangs of a reef.

All fore-and-aft canvas was hauled down; courses, topgallant-sails and royals were furled, and topsails clewed up and left hanging in the buntlines. Then the hatches were raised, and all hands were set to work heaving the rock ballast on deck.

Luckily the ship had touched on a rising tide, what breeze there was blew offshore, and the sounding rod showed that the well was bone dry. At high water it seemed likely that the *Marshall* would float clear, unless the wind chopped around to drive her further into the reef.

While toiling at the winch and hoisting heavy slings of ballast Blake was quite able to appreciate the peaceful loveliness of Fulai. And never had he imagined that Nature could so prodigally endow one spot, even in the rich South Seas, with such redundant charms.

Near the northern headland and nestling under its shelter was a trim white thatched bungalow which overlooked the lagoon. Behind, and stretching over the crest, was the foliage of banana groves, showing that some cultivation at least was to be found here.

Bully Forrester was in charge of the ballast gang. Blake noted that the mate kept gazing shoreward with a queer expression on his rugged, brutal face — an expression that was half conjecture, half reminiscence.

The spilling of a sling of rock, with its consequent damage to the deck, failed to draw more than a quick glance from Forrester; this absence of hot reprisal was so unusual that it attracted Blake's attention to the man.

Even the lowering of the *Foster*'s boats, which indicated a zealous opening of operations, and the volley of oaths from Steelfist, aft, seemed to move the mate but little. Blake, tipping the slings as they came up into a pile on an old tarpaulin, eyed Forrester keenly and became convinced that the mate was no stranger to the place.

While in plain sight, the *Foster* was a good mile away and Blake could not make out any sign of Mary Peabody, as he had half hoped to do. So, as he worked, he directed a quiet question at the mate.

"Know this island, Mr. Forrester?"

The other turned to him with a nod, his rugged features puzzled.

"Know it? You've said it, Dude! Used to know it in the old days — but now it's got me wonderin'."

Blake tipped up a sack with a rattle of rock.

"Yes? Has it changed, then?"

"Some," and a reminiscent chuckle broke from Forrester. "It's near twenty year since I was here — that was in the good days, when a man could load up with black ivory an' get away with it."

"Eh? Black ivory?" Blake looked at him with a swift thought. "Are there natives here, then?"

"Uh-huh. This used to be a good port o' call, Dude. Them fellows were husky scrappers, worth three Kanakas as sailors, fighters, or yam hoers. But when ol' John Wicliff started in to teach 'em things out'n a Boston Bible — bluey! Gin-slingin' traders, glass-bead fakers, an' poor innocent black-birders couldn't scratch a blasted oat here after he begun!"

It was not hard to guess something of Bully Forrester's history from those few words. The mate was a product of the old tough days, and had probably served his apprenticeship to black-birders and the semi-piratical schooner fleets which had been long since cleared from the face of the waters.

"It doesn't look like a very savage place," laughed Blake. "Who's your friend John Wicliff? The same who translated the Bible?"

"I s'pose so," nodded the mate seriously. "I was wonderin' if he was still here or if he'd got chewed up 'fore he converted them blacks. From the looks o' that house, same's as it was twenty year back, he must ha' stuck. Don't see no spears among them lantanas, neither."

"Banana groves mean white men," observed Blake. "So the natives here were a bad lot, I gather?"

"When ol' Wicliff come here, this little island was choke full o' yellin', rippin' savages who'd murder a crew for gin, Dude. The gospel-shark was forty year old when he come, so if he's still here he must be an ol' bird by now. Jupiter! He come with no gun, no square-face, nothin' but a fat Bible."

"He must have been an interesting person," and Blake scanned the apparently deserted island with more interest. "Think he's still around?"

"Mebbe. He's either converted the blacks into Kingdom Come, or they've scoffed him up and them bushes are hoppin' with spears, waitin' for us to land. I'm willin' that Howard should solve the mystery."

The rival skipper seemed to be in no great hurry to get ashore, however. His boats were crawling about the pellucid waters like huge beetles, a man in the bow of each boat taking soundings with a hand lead.

Howard himself directed operations, standing on the *Foster*'s fo'c's'le-head. Mary Peabody was not in evidence.

Now, however, Blake had no further time for observation. The tide was nearing high water mark and the *C. H. Marshall* had to be floated.

Steelfist himself took the deck, and set all three topsails, with yards braced aback. During the next fifteen minutes all hands slaved hard;

ballast was jettisoned, and more ballast was shifted aft in the effort to move the ship.

The backstays curved slack with the strain, while head-stays thrummed in sharp protest; then, with twenty ton of rock gone to buttress the reef, the *Marshall* started astern with a scraping, shivering, grinding slide, and slowly floated clear.

Half an hour later she sailed through the reef entrance, amid a chorused greeting of sarcasm and jeers from Howard's men that set Steelfist's face blacker than a thundercloud. Without reply, the skipper steered her to an anchorage ahead of the *Foster*, in a spot which had not yet been reached by the latter's prowling boats.

Howard's attitude was not long left in doubt. Barely had the cable rust settled on the *Marshall*'s compressor than the rival skipper's boat set forth on an evident visit. Steelfist stood at the rail, watching with a leering scowl, his left hand resting in his jacket pocket.

Ten fathom distant the boat lay to her oars. Howard stood up in the stern-sheets and shook his fist, his massive features working with rage and his entire bull-like appearance eloquent of an overpowering fury.

"You better get your hook an' pull out o' here, Marshall!" he roared. "The first man o' your blasted crowd to set foot ashore gets plugged — you hear me! And if I get my hands on that consarned Finn, I'll toast him over a punk fire. Pull out, my bucko, pull out!"

Steelfist Marshall seemed quite at his ease. He laughed — a grating laugh like the rattle of bones.

"Have you got your title to the island with you, Mr. Slick Howard?" he taunted. "When did you buy Fulai, eh? Sorry, but I got a matter o' business here — private business, it is. As for plugging, you start somethin'. I ain't a bit scared long's you don't come no closer."

His air of quiet raillery passed, and he suddenly leaned forward over the rail, his voice as rage-smitten as that of Howard.

"I'll pull out when I'm good an' ready, see? Now pull out yourself, you —" and he poured a flood of vile abuse at Howard. Every word was an insult, every phase stung like vitriol.

Howard was beyond further speech; his massive features went black with passion. Whipping a pistol from his pocket, he fired on the draw; a tiny crackle of white splinters broke from the rail beside Marshall's steel fist.

The report was echoed instantly, however, by the crack of an automatic in the left hand of Marshall. Howard's weapon flew from his hand and splashed into the sea, while Steelfist grinned.

"I'll learn you to aim straight in a few more lessons, Mr. Howard," he jeered.

"Devil sink you!" roared Howard, dancing in the stern sheets and hanging on to his numbed hand. "It's fight, is it? By jings, you'll have fight, blast you!"

"Chase him off, Mr. Forrester," and Steelfist turned forward. "You can spare a bit more of that ballast, I think."

Forrester nodded. With a whoop of joy the crew caught the idea and flung themselves on the pile of ballast. In five seconds rock was filling the air and all but filling Howard's boat as well.

From her gunwales zipped splinters, and an oar blade split, knocking the loom of the long ash up to the chin of the oarsman and tumbling him among his mates. Howard plumped down in his seat, trying to guard himself with his coat and cursing his men fluently as they made frantic efforts to pull away.

And after them pealed a roar of merriment and defiance from the *Marshall* that wakened echoes from the headlands and the jungle-massed hill of the island.

Since war had thus been formally declared, Steelfist now saw to it that his ship was put in shape to guard against any move from Howard.

With the mates driving all hands, the sails were furled harbor fashion, while another anchor was carried out astern and springs were bent to both cables. Then the ballast was ranged in heaps under the bulwarks, where it would prove efficient ammunition in the event of any attack from the *Foster*'s boats.

Blake was the last man to remain aloft. On his way down he lingered for a moment in the maintop, from which altitude he gained a clear view of the deck of the *Foster*.

As he hung there watching, he saw a small, weazened Chinaman, evidently the steward, emerge from the companionway and cross to the gangway. The steward was bent nearly double under the weight of a small trunk.

Following the steward came a figure which drew an exclamation from Blake.

"The girl! And by George — she must be going ashore!"

So, evidently, she was, since she disappeared by the ladder over the side of the *Foster* opposite Blake. Howard was not in sight. The red-thatched Bingham stood lolling by the rail, watching the girl with half a sneer.

A great relief surged through Blake, for he had feared a dozen things. The *Foster* seemed glad to be rid of Mary Peabody, he observed with no small satisfaction. Possibly their plan had been to lift the treasure and then maroon the girl on the island; but whatever the reason, they seemed to offer no opposition to her leaving.

A moment later Blake caught sight of the boat, shooting out from the *Foster* toward the white bungalow at the north end of the lagoon. Probably, he thought, the girl knew something of the former missionary and intended to occupy the house; then so much the better!

His eyes followed the slight, white-draped figure in the stern of the boat, wistfully enough. Ships, men, island, the very atmosphere of brooding strife — all vanished to Jack Blake as he stood there in the maintop, staring after the boat until his eyes ached with the sun-glare on the glassy water. Before him was her face, piquant, sweet, womanly —

"Aloft there!" rose the raucous bellow of Long Rube Bower. "Want yer bed sent up, Dude?"

Blake slid to the deck and went below.

After dinner, the mate resurrected an ancient diving suit and set to work patching leaky pipes. Long into the afternoon the clean air was polluted by the reek of rubber solution.

The air tubes were bent, battered, worn-out and thoroughly untrustworthy. Blake wondered what man would venture his life under water in such an outfit and said as much to Forrester. The mate grinned evilly.

"You wait an' see, Dude!" and Forrester applied a foot-square patch to a torn knee of the diving suit. "The skipper's got a pleasant way with him, when he wants a thing done, and it ain't easy to refuse, see? I guess it's your job, too."

"You've got another guess coming, then," said Blake quietly, danger in his gray eyes.

He had seen the *Foster*'s boat return without the girl and knew that Mary Peabody was stopping ashore. Therefore, his own problem was to get ashore also and join forces.

"Listen here, Dude," went on Forrester, softly. "I kind o' favor you — an' you know why. Don't you go to rile up the skipper. If he says to dive, you dive; I'll handle the pumps, an' you'll get a square deal, see?"

With that, the mate strode away. Thereafter, as though to make up for his warning, he kept Blake busy on one job after another, until, in the heel of the day, a few natives were descried on the beach opposite the ships. The skipper instantly ordered the cutter dropped over.

Blake ran to the falls, hoping that here was his chance to get ashore and possibly to slip into the jungle and get clear. But in this he was foiled, and by Steelfist Marshall himself.

"You stay aboard," ordered the skipper, laying his hand on Blake's knee, as the latter was climbing over the rail "Quit work, Dude, an' rest up. I'm goin' to try for a couple o' blacks to dive for me. If they can't be got, you'll try your hand at it in the mornin'."

"Not in that rotten suit," and Blake, steadily met Marshall's eyes. "It's rank murder, Captain Marshall! I signed articles as seaman —"

"You go look at them articles," grinned the skipper, only the merest hint of menace in his face. "You're the one man I can trust, Dude, an' you'll go down. Get me?"

Disgusted, Blake went forward, lit his pipe, and sat on the knighthead, moodily staring shoreward. He saw Marshall step on the beach, while the cutter hauled off a few lengths and lay to; then the skipper vanished in the shadow of the jungle into which the natives had darted.

It was plain that the girl had played into the hands of both parties by going ashore; for, with the treasure once salvaged, either Howard or Marshall would seize it and depart, leaving her marooned and out of their way. Nonetheless, she was for the present safe, and presumably with the missionary, Wicliff.

Disturbed by the remembrance of Marshall's grin, Blake slipped down to the forecastle, and, for the first time, perused the copy of the articles tacked to the bulkhead under the ladder. It was a mere sheet of thick paper, eighteen inches by eleven, printed in red; but it constituted the law of the ship, beyond all appeal.

**Office of the U. S. Commissioner
for the port of San Francisco.**

It is agreed between the Master and seamen, or mariners, of the *C. H. Marshall*, of which Charles Marshall is at present Master, or whoever shall go for Master, now bound from the port of San Francisco to Sydney and intermediate ports.

"Hm!" grunted Blake, who had been joined by Fancy Harry Lovell. "Looks as if this phraseology was designed to get the readers mixed up, doesn't it?"

"Well, I dunno 'bout that frasey part of her," rejoined the bo'sun doubtfully, "but I never seen no articles that was easy to understand. The readin' matter is worse mixed up than a law-shark's writin'."

At the scale of provisions, Blake smiled; the low standard set by the law was followed by a list of substitutes left to the discretion of the master. He read aloud the clause enjoining the crew to be orderly, faithful, honest and sober, and a hoarse guffaw from the bunks answered him.

Another guffaw greeted the clause forbidding flogging and corporal punishment under dire penalties; but now, at the bottom, Blake found the joker for which he had been searching.

It is also agreed that, at the discretion of the Master, the crew shall work cargo, load or discharge ballast, perform diving operations, wherever necessary to the successful prosecution of the vessel's business.

With something very like a curse, Blake turned to his bunk.

Whatever he was ordered to do he must do — or suffer the consequences under the articles he had signed. The conviction had come to him that Steelfist Marshall wished him to die, not through any undue confidence, but as a simple means of getting rid of him.

"Then if I'm to get ashore I'd better do it in a hurry," thought Blake. "To blazes with skipper, articles, legality, and everything else! I'd better swim ashore and let the two crews fight out their fight."

He turned over and gripped the revolver, which he had carefully hidden again. Also, he unearthed the contents of Mary Peabody's suitcase, which he had also hidden away after dropping the wreck of the suitcase overboard one night.

Since his only way of deserting seemed to be to swim ashore that night, he made his simple preparations. His revolver and the feminine belongings he rolled up in a scrap of canvas, leaving enough marline loose for a sling, and restowed it under his "donkey's breakfast" — the five-dollar straw tick from the slop chest.

This done, Blake returned on deck and lolled at the rail. The sun was far down the sky, and the masts threw long shadows to the outer reef before the skipper's boat shoved out from shore. Blake noted that another boat, beyond doubt from the *Foster*, lay empty on the beach a hundred yards from Marshall's point of embarkation.

A moment later it was seen that the skipper had been successful in his trip, for two brown figures were huddled in the bows. Yet from the manner in which Marshall urged on his men, he seemed to be in some haste to reach the ship.

This haste was speedily explained — in a fashion that brought Blake to his feet with a startled cry.

From the edge of the jungle near the *Foster*'s boat spat a tiny bluish-white ring of smoke. Steelfist Marshall sprang erect, then sank down with a spasmodic gesture, the report of a rifle cracked over the slumberous trees, and all things relapsed again into quietude.

The boat came on with the sea boiling halfway to her painter-ring under the vivid curses of Marshall. As the skipper came up the gangway, Blake saw that he was livid with more than rage, for a spreading crimson splotch dyed his white linen jacket from shoulder to wrist.

"Take the blacks for'ard," he snarled at the alarmed Forrester and began to peel off his jacket. "That son of a dogfish got to me in my gun arm, blast him! It was Howard, I'll bet my hope o' glory!"

"He went ashore an hour ago, sir," replied the mate. "Hit bad?"

"No. Feels like a flesh puncture, no more. That cursed Howard always was a bad shot, even with a rifle! Best thing is, I've snaffled the only two boys on the island who'll dive. That's spiked him!"

"Where's the Gospel-shark!" inquired Long Rube, assisting in tying up the wound.

"The blacks said he'd prob'ly come out to see me. I told 'em to warn him off my ship, blast him! Come on below, an' get this thing fixed."

Four bells clanged out, and Blake slipped to the fo'c's'l'e, only to snatch a biscuit and a hunk of salt beef and return to the deck. Perching on the rail, he watched the gathering dusk along the shore, fastening every point in his mind; he was by this time quite resolved on "skipping the ship" that night.

A hail from the mate startled him. Turning, he saw a small, slim craft, manned by four rowers, coming from the north end of the lagoon. In the stern Blake could make out a bareheaded figure, whose long white hair flew loose on the wind.

"Now we'll have some fun," leered Forrester, turning toward the companionway. "If there's anythin' the Ol' Man likes, it's them hymn-singers!"

And, with a wink toward Blake, he emitted a roar for Captain Marshall.

CHAPTER X

A CHANGE OF BASE

When the old missionary reached the deck Jack Blake felt a painful sense of comparison between his figure and that of the man who faced him.

For all its weight of years, Wicliff's gaunt frame was as erect as the *Marshall*'s mainmast. His face was bronzed, deeply wrinkled; very strong and steady blue eyes gazed from beneath deep white brows; his entire bearing bespoke a kindly power, a benevolent despotism, as of one who serves a master not to be denied or questioned.

Glancing over the rail, Blake noted that the four natives were unarmed, but were gigantic in stature, sitting motionless like bronze statues.

Marshall came down the deck toward Wicliff, pausing only to snap a curt order at Bower to keep the two diving boys out of sight. Then he faced his visitor.

"Well, mister, what can I do for you?"

There was nothing complacent in his attitude, and Blake foresaw trouble in the wolfish face.

"I am John Wicliff, teacher of the Word of God in this island, sir," began the old man, his voice deep and vibrant, and his steady eyes quite fearless. "I have come —"

"Oh, I know who you are, and all about you," broke in Steelfist Marshall with a sneer. He seemed quite unawed by the patriarchal mien of the missionary. "You're the tub-thumpin' hymn singer as put this place on th' everlastin' blink for trade! I know who you are, all right, and I can't say I like you overmuch. What d'you want o' *me*? That's what I'm askin' ye!"

Blake quietly edged nearer to the poop, a deep anger rising within him. The old man looked at Marshall without resentment; a shade of sorrow rested in his eyes, but no more.

"Brother, you mistake," he returned gently. "I have not fought trade, but only disease and vice. These natives of mine —"

The skipper took a step forward.

"You tell me what you want aboard my ship, and look sharp, mister man! I want none o' your slimy talk."

Wicliff drew himself up, giving Marshall a flash from his quick blue eyes.

"I want nothing, sir, except to ask that you will respect the peace and the tranquility of my people. Not for many years have they heard shots fired with murderous intent, as they have today; the few that are left are peace-loving converts, and my children.

"Now, Captain Marshall, one thing more. I have spoken to Captain

Howard today. I know his errand here, and yours. I may save you much labor and strife by informing you that all your work here will be in vain, since there is absolutely nothing in this lagoon worth fighting for or working for. That is what I came to say, sir."

As he listened to this frank speech Marshall's evil passion blazed forth more wolfishly than ever, and his right arm went back.

Blake, gripping the manrope of the poop ladder, set foot on the lower step, every muscle tensed. Were Marshall brutal enough to attack this old man —

"You listen here!" snarled Steelfist threateningly. "You've ruined enough men here, with your damned Bible palaver and your complaints to the gunboat patrol. I know you, blast you, and I'll go to Tophet if you'll buy chips in my game!

"So Howard got to you first, did he? Curse his ugly mug — he's payin' you to hand out that dope to me, I s'pose! He'll pay you with the end of the mainsheet, and that's your own funeral, my old buck. But you won't play loose with Steelfist Marshall, savvy that? You swim home, quickest you know! Bower — pitch the old bone-rack over the side! Lively!"

Long Rube leaped forward, wrapped his huge arms about the unresisting Wicliff, and bore back the old man to the rail. In ten seconds his grip relaxed, and he staggered away under a stunning blow on the ear.

Blake, his gray eyes blazing with fury, followed up his first lead with a straight right-and-left that sent the second mate reeling again.

Wicliff stood at the rail, gaunt and fearless, refusing to take advantage of the opening to reach his boat.

The second officer fought back viciously, but could not stand before the silent, furious attack of Blake. The latter drove Bower steadily back, sending home blow after blow, worked the man against the wheel and then measured his distance for the finishing uppercut.

But that decisive drive never went home.

Marshall, waiting only until Blake stood steady for a moment, poised that terrible right arm and crashed his steel fist squarely into Blake's temple, felling him like a log.

"Over with him, Forrester!" the skipper snarled.

John Wicliff was hurled clumsily into the sea, to be picked up an instant later by his own natives, in whose bronze faces simmered lowering hatred. They turned about and were lost in the gathering darkness, sending back a single long yell.

When Blake recovered his senses he found himself lying on the main hatch, his wrists and feet lashed down with small rope. The decks were in semi-darkness, for night had settled on the ship, and during a long space Blake stared up at the blazing stars and cursed everything in general and his own temper in particular.

That savage outburst had only served to work harm upon himself;

he did not consider that it might yet have more momentous consequences. His temple throbbed with a heavy ache and his entire skull felt as though it had been ripped from chin to crown.

"I was a fool to let go of myself that way," he reflected bitterly. "I couldn't help old Wicliff, and only got in Dutch myself! Now, two to one, Steelfist will send me down in that diving dress tomorrow and then cut the air-hose. I suppose he means to find the wreck by soundings —"

What was it that Wicliff had said — that there was nothing in the lagoon? At this thought, Blake stiffened in his bonds.

Mary Peabody had sought Wicliff's protection, beyond doubt. And so sincere and grave was the old man's very atmosphere that the girl must have opened her heart to him. Therefore, if there had ever been a wreck in the lagoon, it must now either have been washed out or broken up by the surf.

However that might be, Blake was well aware that his own position was now serious in the extreme. His hard-won standing had been swept away by a moment's anger, and in the morning he could expect to face the wolfish cruelty of Marshall. A twist at his lashings told him he had no hope of escape.

The only man on deck seemed to be a dim figure aft, but Blake's nostrils caught the lazy curl of a pipe, and he guessed that he was by no means alone. This was verified an instant later when a heavy step thudded behind him.

Then, to his surprise, a hand touched his aching head and he caught a low whisper.

"Ay t'ink ju t'irsty, huh?"

An arm slipped under his neck, raising his head, while a pannikin of water was placed to his lips, and he looked up into the pale blue eyes of Ole Kafban. The Finn sat down while helping Blake drink.

"Ju should better cl'ar out, Ay t'ink. Dey vos yolly sore mit ju."

"So I understand," chuckled Blake grimly. "Do you want to come and help Miss Peabody, too?"

"Ay not shwim," came the stolid answer. "Ju want me cut ju free?"

Blake was already calculating. There was no danger of discovery, it seemed, and he was anxious to get hold of his bundle.

"Not yet," he said, as the Finn slipped out his knife. "Go down and fetch me the canvas bundle that's in my bunk. Then if any one examines me while you're gone they'll suspect nothing."

Ole nodded and slid away into the darkness.

For a moment Blake lay straining every sense. He heard no sound at all, yet he had a feeling that some one else was close at hand; suddenly he caught his breath sharply as something cold touched his wrists.

"Will ye keep quiet now?" came a warning whisper in the voice of Paddy Ryan.

Blake felt a knife slit through his lashings; then Paddy sank down, till his mouth was against Blake's ear.

"Careful, Dude — the mate's aft. Slip over the side — ain't no sharks here. Them two divers has gone; they heard the blacks yell when the ol' gent was hove over, an' swum for it. Good luck, ol' hoss!"

Before Blake could answer he felt his hands pressed in a quick grip, then Paddy Ryan was gone.

Lying quiet, stretching his cramped hands to restore the circulation, Blake thanked Heaven for the two friends who had come to aid him at this crisis — even though he laughed silently at the fashion in which each had come to complement the help of the other.

The next instant his hands closed on something hard — a pipe and a slab of fine tobacco. He was not ashamed of the tears which sprang to his eyes in that moment; for these were the treasures of Paddy Ryan, the costliest gifts which he could offer to a departing friend.

"Please God, I'll some day repay the debt I owe Paddy Ryan!" Blake told himself.

Thus, when Ole Kafban padded back to him, he rose up and laid hands upon the Finn, sending the man into trembling fright.

"All right," he whispered reassuringly. "I got loose, Ole. Did you get it?"

"H'ar's bundle," came the answer, "Mabbe ju help Miss Pebbody?"

"I'll try, anyhow," said Blake cheerfully. "Good-by, old man — sorry you can't swim! If you can get ashore later, do so."

"Sure. Ju climb down dot cable-sham, an' dond't stop for notting! Yump — git oud't, now!"

Ole slipped off, evidently seeing no use in running more risks.

Blake silently crept up to the windlass, finding the forward deck quite deserted. Crouching beside the hawse, he tied the bundle securely to his head; then sent a searching glance into the shimmering radiance of the lagoon to get his bearings.

Once sure of these, he slipped down the cable without a sound, slid into the water and quietly struck out.

Before he had gone ten feet he noted with a little shiver of alarm the flashing swirl of phosphorescence eddying behind him. Were a boat sent after him at this stage, he was lost!

Eight bells tinkled out on the stillness, the strokes leaping across the rippling lagoon to wake soft echoes from the jungle and headlands. A moment later the *Foster*'s bell also rang the hour, proving that Howard was awake.

Neither ship had relaxed sea-watches; the feeling between them was too tense to permit either skipper to leave his vessel to the mercies of a single anchor-watch. While Blake knew, from the ease of his own escape, that some might congregate in the galley for a smoke and a game, he felt pretty certain that the watch from the poop would be keen enough.

A moment later his surmise proved all too correct. He was nearing the black shore-reflection and was striking out in fresh confidence, when shouts rang out from the *Marshall* — shouts in which Blake caught the angry tones of Bower and the growl of the mate.

Now, knowing that his only chance lay in getting ashore before a boat picked him up, he sprinted hard, careless of the phosphorescence that betrayed him. Something "plutted" into the water by his head, followed by the sharp crack of a rifle; desperately, he renewed his efforts, not daring to pause to allow the radiance to die away.

A second shot echoed out, but he heard the bullet zipping through the trees. Another few strokes, and the sand rose beneath his feet; in ten seconds he was running up the hard beach into shelter of the bush. There he paused, chuckling.

The shots and cries had aroused the *Foster* to swift suspicion, and over the still lagoon was resounding a wordy war which in detail was less nice than clever. It was evident that there would be little sleep aboard either ship that night.

Blake, who had put his pumps into the bundle, resumed them, took the revolver from the roll also and pocketed it. Then he struck out along the beach to the north, careful to keep in shadow of the lantana fringe, and to watch warily for any sign of too curious natives.

He saw no one, however, and the *Marshall* seemed to have sent out no boats. In ten minutes the light of the mission bungalow gleamed through the bush above, and he cut straight up from the beach toward it. Now that he was within a few yards of meeting the girl who would not pass out of his thoughts, he felt unaccountably embarrassed.

The open veranda of the bungalow was flooded with soft light, but no one seemed to be stationed on watch. The cane screen, rolled up for greater coolness, gave Blake a clear view of the living-room interior.

Two cane lounge chairs faced the doorway. In one sat the white-haired old missionary, reading with untroubled features; in the other, engaged with needle and thread, was Mary Peabody. A lamp-bearing table between them completed the picture, and Blake gazed at it with a lump in his throat.

In neither face was there worry or trouble — the girl looked up to Wicliff with a word and a flashing smile, and the old man nodded placidly. Somewhat ashamed of his prying, Blake stepped up to the veranda, dripping water at every step, and stood in the open doorway.

"Good evening," he said quietly, smiling as he spoke. "I hope that you're still receiving callers, Mr. Wicliff?"

With a swift little cry of alarm the girl dropped her work, staring at the door. But, without surprise, the gaunt missionary rose and advanced, hand extended, as though to greet some well-known and very welcome visitor.

"Good evening, sir, and welcome to you!" he said. As their hands met the two men looked each other in the eye for a moment; and if there was admiration in the gaze of Blake, it was fully repaid in the piercing blue eyes of the old man.

"My name is John Blake," said the American quietly, holding up his bundle and tossing it to the table. "I've just come from the *C. H. Marshall*, and I've brought some things which Miss Peabody will, perhaps, be glad to recover."

The girl was staring at him with a look of puzzled recognition. As he smiled, waiting for her to remember, he noted that her eyes were deep brown, that she was rather a woman than a girl, and that in her bearing was a note of capability and efficiency which bespoke the blood of old Captain Peabody of clipper-ship days. She was well poised, thought Blake.

"Why —" and the girl rose, putting out her hand, her eyes steadily on his, "aren't you the gentleman who — who did me a very great service that night by the Custom House back in 'Frisco?"

"I had that honor," and Blake laughed as their hands gripped. "Unfortunately, I did not know about Captain Marshall's steel fist until he made me painfully aware of it, and then shanghaied me —"

"And," broke in Wicliff's deep, severe voice, "this is the man of whom I told you, Miss Peabody — the same who made that luckless but very gallant effort to save me from rough handling this afternoon. Sit down, Mr. Blake — I gather that you have swum ashore from the ship?"

Blake, blushing, became acutely conscious of his extremely disreputable garb and general appearance.

"If you'll be good enough to lend me some decent clothes," he said, turning, "I'll venture to ask your hospitality for some time to come. I'm afraid my late quarters are too hot to hold me —"

"My dear fellow, I beg your pardon!" exclaimed Wicliff, taking his arm. "Excuse us, Miss Peabody! Come along, Blake; I've plenty of room here, and — hello! You've a nasty bruise there! Well, it can wait till we return."

Blake followed his host to a small, immaculate bedroom, where Wicliff got out a razor and some white clothes. Despite the ragged bruise on his temple, in twenty minutes Blake looked and felt like a new man; he was free, all the enforced humility of ordinary seaman was sloughed, and he was again the Jack Blake of old.

Yet not the same, he realized as he inspected himself in the mirror. His face was indefinably older and grimmer, set in steadier lines, stamped with the seal of strife and hard living; it had gained in strength, if not in beauty, he reflected. Then, looking at his hands, he held them out to Wicliff with a laugh.

"I thought a few months ago that I had strong hands — but look at them now! Brine and holystones and tarred ropes combine to make a poor manicure, eh? By the way, I gather that you know Miss Peabody's story?"

"Yes," nodded the old man, gravely. "And I knew her grandfather twenty years and more ago, before his ship broke over that outer reef. Now — all ready?"

They returned to the living-room and Blake, a smile transforming his hard-chiseled features, walked up to the girl.

"I feel like being introduced all over again," he laughed. "I haven't been so presentable since the first time we met, Miss Peabody!"

"Well, you certainly have changed in the last few moments," she agreed, with a twinkle of appreciation in her eye.

Wicliff had gone to a large sandalwood chest and was bending over it.

The girl touched the bundle, which lay where Blake had tossed it.

"Did you mean to say that this was mine?" she asked, puzzled.

Blake nodded, unknotting the marline.

"Yes — the contents of your suitcase. You see, Marshall kidnapped Ole Kafban at Honolulu. I was able to kidnap the suitcase on my own hook and managed to keep its contents intact and out of sight. Your friend Ole is a mighty good man, by the way; it was owing to him that I got free tonight."

"I'm glad Ole is safe," she answered, watching the bundle in astonishment as Blake unrolled it. "The poor fellow tried to be kind to me — though Captain Howard swore that he had stolen my suitcase and joined your ship."

Wicliff stood up and set a flask and roll of linen on the table.

"Now for your head, Blake," he said. "Sit down, and we'll soon have you fixed up; meantime, you might give us an outline of your story. There seem to be a good many things that need explaining — such as the revolver in your pocket, for instance."

Blake started. He had thought that he had transferred the weapon to his white coat without being observed, and the implied rebuke did not escape him.

"That revolver may prove to be a good friend yet," he returned, as he sat down. "Well, no matter. Here's the gist of my yarn, Miss Peabody."

And so he related his experience, and Mary Peabody's brown eyes compelled more of his tale, perhaps., than he had thought to tell.

CHAPTER XII

A SUDDEN BREAK TO PEACE

"There are a few things I'm anxious to know myself," said Blake, when he had made an end of his story. "Why, for instance, did you not stop ashore at Honolulu, Miss Peabody? Had you not realized Howard's villainy at that time?"

The girl nodded gravely.

"Yes. But I had to pay him in advance for my charter, and — and — well, Mr. Blake, I simply had no more money. Everything depended on this voyage for me, as I knew that my grandfather had the savings of a lifetime with him when he was wrecked; the location of the wreck I got from my father, who in turn had received it from one of the few survivors."

"And has no one ever looked for it since?" exclaimed Blake, in surprise.

At the question he saw a swift look pass between the missionary and Mary Peabody, and as the girl hesitated, he continued swiftly.

"I beg your pardon — I was not trying to pry into your secret. Let's forget the whole subject of treasure, anyway. Mr. Wicliff, I trust that you don't mind sheltering me for the present?"

"Most assuredly not," smiled the old man, and Blake noted again the piercing keenness of the blue eyes. "And Miss Peabody will lose nothing if my poor efforts can prevent it. So the two ships are at odds, eh?"

"Something of the sort," laughed Blake. "Each crew is determined to cheat each other, each hates each other like the devil hates holy water, and I don't think they would need the incentive of treasure to be at each other's throats. By the way, are your natives armed? Can you resist any attempt at landing?"

Wicliff shook his head somberly.

"No. And I am deeply grieved that, after many years of peace, my little vineyard must again witness the strife of brutal men. When I came here, the island held a population of a thousand or more — perhaps the most vicious savages in the south seas. Now, I am glad to say, there are but twelve men left."

Blake stared, incredulous; then wondered if he had heard aright.

"Eh?" he exclaimed sharply. "You mean twelve hundred?"

"No," and Wicliff smiled. "I mean twelve. They are young, each has a wife, and the little ones have not a bodily blemish. Perhaps you do not understand the terrible effects of vice and iniquity in these latitudes, Mr. Blake?"

"There are a good many things I'm ignorant of," and Blake leaned back in wonder. "I can't see why you're glad that you have twelve parishioners instead of a thousand."

Mary Peabody laughed.

"Don't you see — Mr. Wicliff has for twenty years presided over an experiment in eugenics, so to speak! And now he's succeeded in starting a new race, practically, which will be twice as good as the old one. Isn't that right?"

Wicliff nodded soberly. "Yes, and before I am called away I trust that I shall see the village in the way of sturdy growth again."

His voice vibrant with the kindly wisdom of his years, he spoke of his work here in Fulai; and as he listened, Jack Blake as never before realized how he himself, with his polo and motorcars and wealth, was nothing in the face of such a man as this John Wicliff, whose whole life had spelled service.

Wicliff told of his twenty years of patient labor, his struggles against a warlike population rendered hostile to him by the wiles and liquor of traders. He spoke of the ravages made by disease and drunkenness among the natives, how scores of them had been black-birded, how their fearless and free spirit had been all but crushed as their numbers had decreased more alarmingly each year.

"But at last," concluded Wicliff, "the authorities stepped in and forced the traders and slavers to leave us in peace. Now, thank God, those who are left are clean in body and soul; my reward has come in the love and trust which they repose in me, and this has made the struggle well worth while."

The missionary fell silent, staring down at the floor. Mary Peabody was watching him with so rapt a face that Jack Blake caught his breath suddenly; never had he thought to see such expression on the face of a woman as he surprised on hers in that moment.

"What did you put on my head?" he asked and felt almost guilty as he saw the girl's face change. "It has taken the pain out, and the swelling is certainly going down fast!"

"A native ointment," said Wicliff, rousing himself from his daydreams. "These natives were very warlike, as I said, and they had many such preparations. I have found them very good."

Blake nodded.

"And now," he said quietly, "I hope that you and Miss Peabody will accept my services and assistance? It was for that purpose I left the ship, and I cannot return. I'm very much afraid that our troubles are not yet ended."

The girl rose and extended her hand to him, her gaze holding his with a steadiness that was almost disconcerting.

"Thank you, Mr. Blake. And I want you to know that I am deeply grateful, both for your trouble and kindness in bringing my things, and for your earlier service at San Francisco — the cause of all your own troubles. Now I think I'll say good night, and we'll see you in the morning."

Blake smiled, and again his hard-lined face was transformed into that tenderness for which many women love some men.

"Your friendship and trust are higher payment than I had ever hoped to find, Miss Peabody. Good night, and pleasant dreams!"

She vanished, and Blake turned as Wicliff's hand fell on his shoulder.

"My son," and the old man's eyes bit deep, "you are a man — aye, such a man as I would wish to call my son in all truth! Now, for the present you had best occupy a hammock on the veranda at night, and for tomorrow at least remain out in the bush, lest your skipper come in search of you. My natives will care for and watch over you, never fear."

"Thank you," responded Blake, surprised anew by the strength of the wrinkled hand that gripped his. "And you'll arm your boys, I suppose?"

"Not for the present — God forbid! I have means to protect Miss Peabody for a little while, I think. Now come along, and sleep secure."

Five minutes later Blake rolled into a hammock slung on the veranda. He was asleep almost at once; but before he dropped off, he looked out at the starlit lagoon and made one remark to the riding light of the *Marshall*.

"By the Lord, she's a *woman!*"

At sunrise Blake breakfasted with Mary Peabody and Wicliff, finding that no movement had been noted aboard the two ships.

Since it was certain that Steelfist Marshall would not passively accept the desertion of Blake, following that of the two natives, Wicliff determined to adopt precautionary measures at once.

Much against her wish, Mary Peabody was sent off with two of the natives to the village, located two miles back in the bush toward the opposite side of the island. Here she would remain out of harm's way for the present. Wicliff himself would stay at the bungalow; the missionary stated rightly enough that he had little to fear, with his natives in the bush to protect the approaches.

Before the morning grew hot two natives took Blake up beyond the bungalow to the crest of the northern headland. Here he found a small grass hut at the edge of the banana groves, from which the entire lagoon and a half-moon of beach lay in plain view.

Before the natives vanished they also showed Blake a path leading to the village, but out of sight from the ships below. He ensconced himself comfortably with binoculars and basket of food and prepared to watch operations.

His view was beautiful in the extreme, and he had small thought for the passing of time. Below him, the reef-heads revealed themselves pale-green under the swells which held the blackness of immense depth farther out; and, deeply though he detested the ships in the lagoon, despite his soul-dwarfing experiences with them, his heart could not but leap to the picture they presented.

They were just distant enough to be rid of blemishes. The rusty black sides, streaked by weeks of seafaring, gleamed in the morning glow like polished ebony. The stained and splintered rails set off the black hulls like lines of flashing ivory. Even in the verdigris-green brass work of binnacles, bells, pole-compasses and skylight gratings, the searching sunlight picked out shining metal that gleamed up at him in blinding brilliance.

And, towering high into the vastly deep of the blue sky, the masts became streaks of gold, ruled with flashing threads of cob-webbery and crossed by other golden streaks whereon the slovenly-furled sails lay like spotless snow.

With the full day, however, came teeming activity aboard the two ships. Boats were put out and began flitting over the lagoon; evidently both skippers were making search for the wreck. One boat, however, made a straight course for the bungalow, and through his glasses Blake saw Steelfist Marshall in her stern.

Running up the beach, the boat landed and Marshall vanished toward the bungalow, which was just out of Blake's range of vision. For half an hour nothing happened; then Marshall reappeared, plainly in a towering rage, and drove his men out with curses that reached Blake's ears.

Noon came and passed almost unnoticed by the watching Blake.

In some anxiety as to the result of that visit, Blake finally leaped up and started down the path leading to the bungalow. As he did so, however, a bronze and grinning native stepped from the tangle of bush, holding up one hand in token of peace; at the man's back was slung a wicked shark-tooth spear.

The man had been one of his guides, Blake remembered.

"No 'fraid, only me!" said the native in a mellow voice.

"Glad to see you," laughed Blake. "Where's Mr. Wicliff? Is he all right?"

"All ri', all ri', you no 'fraid! Stop along alla same I show you — bimeby come miss'nary papa. You stop?"

Blake nodded, reassured, and returned to his hut.

Now he observed that the questing boats were fast falling foul of each other, and at the far side of the lagoon two of the small craft were engaged in a fast and furious oar fight.

"Hello!" chuckled Blake. "There's the red-headed Bingham — bet a dollar he falls foul of Forrester — ah, I thought so!"

Sure enough, Bingham's boat had fouled the bows of Bully Forrester's cutter. The two mates drew an oar's length distant from each other and evidently began to exchange compliments.

A moment later something flashed from Bingham's boat, and one of Forrester's men fell and lay limply across the thwart. With a mad dipping of oars, the two boats came together.

"Poor fellows — and all for nothing!" exclaimed a pitying voice.

Blake whirled and saw John Wicliff standing at his shoulder, watching the lagoon with sorrowful eyes. Turning again to the water, Blake leaned forward in excitement, every nerve taut.

"Look at that!" he exclaimed. "It's rank murder — God!"

Oars, boathooks and stretchers were flashing between the two boat crews in murderous play. But Forrester had risen in the stern, out of the mêlée, the coiled lead line in his left hand.

Twice the sounding-lead whirled around his head, then he loosed it with deadly aim. The plummet took Bingham squarely over the ear; the red-haired mate of the *Foster* went down and lay motionless.

Then the *Foster*'s men pulled out of the combat, pursued by taunting yells. But Blake knew that one man had died this day.

He was human enough to care little how far this work went among the two crews; he was human enough to care a great deal for Wicliff and the little flock of natives; but when he looked into the eyes of the patriarch, Jack Blake realized that this man had a spirituality, a common humanity with all things, such as he himself would never know.

"All is well with us, Blake," said Wicliff quietly. "Marshall visited me, and I gave him no satisfaction. Two of my boys were repairing their spears, and the tacit warning reached him. He went away cursing you."

"Curses come home to roost," laughed Blake "Good for you! By the way, just where is the wreck of Peabody's ship? They seem to be quartering the lagoon without much success."

Wicliff smiled and pointed to the reef.

"She broke up at the false entrance, just here under us, where your ship grounded. She never got safe inside, but was swept over the reef after striking and sank immediately. She must have broken her back when she struck."

"Hm!" mused Blake. "Then they'll find her sooner or later, eh?"

"I suppose so," and Wicliff nodded. "Now, for the present, you had better stay here night and day, Blake. Miss Peabody is remaining at the village, also. I'll have your hammock brought up and slung here."

"But —"

"No objections, please!" Wicliff's blue eyes flashed sternly as he gazed at the ships below. "I want to avoid all strife as far as possible and want to keep my little band of natives intact. So farewell until tomorrow — you'll be kept supplied with food and water."

Wicliff departed, and Blake resigned himself to patience.

With the next morning a body, evidently that of Bingham, was slid overboard from the *Foster* with scant ceremony. As the boats put out again, Blake wondered that Howard did not attempt reprisals — then saw the reason and chuckled.

Long Rube Bower was in the maintop of the *Marshall*, armed with a rifle; since he had complete command of the *Foster*'s decks, it was evident that for the present a state of armed peace would ensue.

Nor were there further conflicts between the boat crews, though enough of bad language and threatening overtures were exchanged. All that day the boats swept the lagoon with lead lines, working gradually toward the head of the lagoon where lay the false entrance, but finding nothing.

Watching their progress, Blake could make out Cutlip Sullivan and Young Boston in one of the *Foster*'s boats, while Keough seemed to be serving as bo'sun aboard Howard's ship. Plainly, the three men were better content there than under Steelfist Marshall.

Although natives appeared with food for him, Blake gained no word of Wicliff or Mary Peabody that day, save that he was to "stop along here one time — miss'nary papa all ri'! White Mary all ri'!" And so the night fell, and Blake swung into his hammock, confident that the natives were watching all that went on in the lagoon.

With the next morning Forrester appeared in the *Marshall*'s rigging, his rifle holding a menace over the *Foster*. But still Howard seemed content to make no overt move, merely sending out his boats to continue quartering the lagoon.

Knowing as he did the exact location of the wreck, providing there were anything left of it, Blake kept his glasses trained with growing interest. It was plain that both crews were watching each other narrowly, as the boats gradually drew into the head of the lagoon, almost under Blake's cranny.

"Getting close!" thought Blake, toward noon. "If they find nothing, they're apt to come ashore after Mary Peabody for further information. And that means trouble."

Eight bells rang out, and the boats returned for the noon meal. Half an hour later the *Marshall*'s boats again put out for the north end of the lagoon. The crew of the *Foster* tumbled over also, but there seemed to be a delay; then the *Foster*'s forecastle sprang into sudden activity, her boats lined out ahead, and Blake saw that they had taken hawsers from the ship.

"Found it!" he ejaculated, seizing his glasses. "Howard's a slick one, right enough! And he's got the lead on Marshall!"

As the *Foster* began to move in tow of her boats, those from the *Marshall* came racing in — Steelfist, in charge of them, evidently realizing that Howard had located the wreck in the course of the morning.

Drive his men though he would, Steelfist was far behind. The *Marshall* had barely begun to move when the *John Foster* dropped anchor immediately opposite and just inside the false entrance of the reef.

"He found it all right," thought Blake. "That's exactly where Wicliff said the wreck had washed over!"

Steelfist Marshall crowded his ship in beside the *Foster* — so close that they had barely room to swing to their anchors.

Almost underneath the headland as they were, everything aboard the two ships was distinct and clear to Blake; he could pick out every man aboard the *Marshall* by some familiar peculiarity of gait or figure.

No sooner were the ships moored than there was a bustle and a glint of metal on both decks, as diving-pumps were rigged and suits made ready.

Big Frank Keough went down for the *Foster*; and, with a feeling of helpless wrath, Blake saw Ole Kafban forced to don the antiquated harness of the *Marshall*. Bully Forrester took charge of the pumps, however, and Blake realized that Steelfist was no doubt trying the apparatus on the Finn with a view to sending down a better man later.

Darkness put an end to the operations, however, and before the clank of pumps had ceased both divers regained their ships safely. Since no hostilities were in evidence, Blake conjectured that a truce had been arranged by tacit consent; it was folly to waste men over nothing, and it would be time enough to fight when either skipper had something to fight for.

Concluding that there was for the present no danger at all, Blake determined to return to the house and, possibly, go on to the native village where Mary Peabody was domiciled. When the native appeared with his supper of fish and taro wrapped in leaves, Blake turned to him with this resolve.

"Where's Mr. Wicliff? He stop along house?"

"He all ri'," grinned the native with exasperating complacency. "Miss'nary papa say you stop along here one time."

"Well, look see," rejoined Blake. "You speak miss'nary papa that I'm coming to the house, savvy? Where's Miss Peabody?"

"White Mary all ri'."

Blake grunted. Evidently he could extract nothing.

"You savvy bad fella down there?" and he pointed to the ships and lagoon.

"Savvy all ri'," and the native, with a grin, touched his shark-tooth spear. "We fix 'um. No 'fraid!"

"Run along then, and be a good boy," laughed Blake, his ill-humor unable to stand before the cheerful grins of the native. "Speak miss'nary papa that I'm coming to the house tonight. I want to see him and Miss Peabody too. You savvy that?"

"Savvy all ri'," nodded the native, and with a flash of teeth turned about and was gone.

Blake ate his supper and then, lighting the pipe which Paddy Ryan had left with him, started off for the bungalow.

He paid no attention to the warning which the native had conveyed. Wicliff, he considered, was striving hard to maintain peace and probably wanted him safe out of the way.

This, however, was by no means to Blake's notion of the fitness of things. There seemed to be no danger for the present from either Howard or Marshall, and — the brown eyes of Mary Peabody argued away all objections in Blake's mind.

Upon reaching the bungalow, he found it dark and evidently deserted. The place seemed almost unnaturally quiet. When he stepped to the veranda and called no answer came, and Blake wondered if there were any one on guard near by.

"Well, I'll finish my pipe," he reflected, drawing a chair near the steps and settling down. "If no one shows up by that time, I'll strike out for the village and see what I can see!"

So, for a space, he rested in comfort, listening to the rustling and sighing of the breeze in the jungle. Then, as he knocked out his pipe he stiffened suddenly at a voice which seemed startlingly close.

"Watch them rats, Bower! Come along, you blasted skunks!"

It was the voice of Steelfist Marshall. Before Blake could more than grip the revolver in his pocket, he saw the dim, shadowy figures of a half dozen men crowding from the path into the edge of the clearing. There they halted, vague in the starlight.

From the lantanas came a whisper and a rustle. The men with Marshall cried out in swift alarm, and the skipper cursed vividly.

"Arrows — the devil! What in hell —"

"Look out!" sounded Bower's voice quickly. "They're beatin' it, cap'n! Git out o' here quick, or we're gone! Poison —"

That word of itself stampeded them, and Marshall's curses died out as he followed hastily. From the lantanas came a guttural ripple of laughter, though no figures appeared in the clearing.

Blake chuckled, his tensed muscles relaxing. Steelfist's night raid had ended in blind panic, for it was plain that the arrows had done no harm; but Blake was now well assured that the natives were keeping good watch.

Curious to see the result of that panic, he stepped to the ground and strode off along the path to the beach. If Marshall were gathering his forces for a second effort, thought Blake, he could make himself useful.

It soon proved, however, that Steelfist and his men had no stomach for such work at night. As Blake reached the edge of the bush and stepped out to the strip of beach he chuckled again at sight of the trail of phosphorescence left by Marshall's cutter, which was heading for the ship at full speed.

Delighted with the cool sweetness of the shore, Blake got put his pipe again and began to fill it, walking along the fringe of lantanas.

"There'll be no more night raids from the *C. H. Marshall*," he reflected. "And for tomorrow, at least, they'll be busy diving. I wish I could get Ole ashore! Still, he's not a fighting man, and these natives seem to be efficient enough in their own way — hello! What's this?"

At the water's edge lay a mass of tangled wreckage — palms and bush, perhaps driven up by some storm from the reef or the other end of the lagoon. As Blake came to it he noted a dark shape just behind; it proved to be a ship's boat, drawn up on the sand, and deserted. Probably it had been hidden from the sight of Marshall.

As Blake halted, staring at it, he heard a sudden laugh, and turned. But as he did so, a figure crashed into him, another figure fell bodily upon him and bore him face downward into the sand, and he heard a rush of feet.

So sudden was the attack that to fight back was impossible. As Blake went down hands caught his arms and ankles, and he felt himself wrapped with rope. A foul-smelling rag was wound about his mouth, and a moment later he was flung roughly into the boat, which scraped over the sand to the water.

"Gotcher, huh?" rambled a voice in his ear — the voice of Cutlip Sullivan. "Now ye'll pay fer that lickin' ye give me, my bucko! Ye'll get plain hell aboard the *Foster*, an' it's me what'll give it to ye, see?"

CHAPTER XIII
HOWARD'S VENGEANCE

"Who ye got there, Jackson?"

Howard's voice sang out as the boat swung in to the *John Foster*. Jackson, formerly second officer and now mate, vice Bingham, seemed to be in command of the shore party, for he answered at once from somewhere near Blake. But his tones were cautious.

"We got their star fighter, the Dude, sir. Go easy till we get him up — hoist away quietly, there! No use tellin' the *Marshall* all our business."

It was plain to Blake that the later developments of his own story were unknown to those aboard the *Foster*, who knew only what Sullivan, Keough and Boston had told them after leaving Honolulu. And that tale had lost nothing in the telling.

Five minutes later Blake was dragged to the poop, promising himself that at some future day he would richly repay the kicks with which Sullivan regaled him *en route*. He found the mate reporting to Howard, and his gag was stripped off, then his foot lashings removed.

"He was skulkin' in the bush, like he was dodgin' Marshall," said Jackson, who had an Irish-cockney whine to him. "Make him talk, sir —"

"You shut your head an' go below," broke in Howard. "You men git for'ard an' keep an eye on that blasted Marshall! I'll 'tend to this man."

Howard was obeyed promptly. Blake followed the skipper's beckoning finger aft, and was told to sit down on the wheel-gratings. Howard stood leaning on the wheel-box, massive and dominant, eying Blake as closely as the uncertain starlight would permit.

"So you're the bully who's raised so much hell aboard the *Marshall*, eh?" he asked thoughtfully.

Blake, who had been mentally kicking himself for his stupidity in being caught napping, held his peace. Howard's manner was anything but hostile, and his next words gave Blake a very definite notion of the ideas working behind his massive features.

"I hear you licked Steelfist, son. That's goin' some, single-handed. Mebbe you ain't in love with him, specially?"

"We aren't exactly bosom friends," returned Blake dryly. "He shanghaied me in San Francisco, for one thing. For another, he gave me a nice bump with his steel hand the other day — a little love-tap I'd like to return with interest."

Instantly Blake saw that he had adopted the right attitude. Howard grinned.

"If you pull with me you'll get the chanct, Dude! His rats have killed my mate, and this time's goin' to be his finish — he's butted in on my voyages long enough. Now, how about it? Want to ship?"

"Not particularly." Blake felt his ground cautiously now, convinced that Howard wanted a fighting recruit more than a hostage. "I don't care a snap about either of you, Howard. Marshall's out to find this treasure, and I gather that you're out to cheat Miss Peabody if you can, ahead of Marshall. Isn't that the way it lies?"

Howard stroked his big jowl reflectively.

"No, I can't say it is," he returned slowly. "So that cursed Finn has been tellin' tales about things, huh? Let's see, now. Why might you think I'm out to cheat the girl, Dude?"

Here was a skipper with more brains than Marshall, thought Blake. He was not at all deceived in the matter; but, convinced that he was now fighting for more than his own safety alone, he followed Howard's lead cautiously.

"General principles, Howard. We learned a few things from the Finn, of course, and Miss Peabody seemed mighty anxious to leave your ship."

"Huh! You ain't seen her, ashore?"

"I tried to hard enough," and Blake grinned to himself. "But she wasn't in sight around the house, and your men nabbed me before I got farther."

All of which was essentially true, and drew another grunt of satisfaction from the bull-like skipper, who plainly thought that he had measured up his captive at last.

"Listen here," and Howard leaned forward earnestly. "Miss Peabody chartered my ship to come here, see? I ain't playin' against her none whatever — I'm buckin' Marshall's game. He's the guy that's tryin' to cheat her. Ain't you willin' to stand up an' fight fer a skirt, Dude?"

"If Miss Peabody's business is safe with you," rejoined Blake promptly, "then set me free and count me in to whip Marshall. I've skipped his ship, and I'm willing to help secure Miss Peabody's interests. That's all I have to say."

"And it's enough for me, my bucko." With a great show of candor Howard caught Blake's wrists and loosened the rope. "Your name's Blake, ain't it? Well, I don't want you puttin' any o' my bullies out o' commission, and Bingham's gone — damn that Forrester! We want fighters, not seamen. You'll live aft an' rank as actin' second mate."

"That suits me," said Blake quietly.

Howard nodded as if well pleased, and led Blake to a berth off the cabin, after which he resumed the deck.

"Not so bad!" reflected the new second officer of the *John Foster*. "You didn't fool me a little bit, Cap'n Slick Howard! I'll spring a big surprise on you one of these days — and meantime, I'd better rest up while I can."

Whereupon Jack Blake rolled into his berth, chuckled anew at the "slickness" of the astute Captain Howard, and fell asleep.

He could not afford to worry over the anxiety his absence might cause Wicliff, and knew that his whereabouts would soon be descried from shore by the missionary. All things considered, it was a stroke of luck which had brought about his presence on the *Foster*; especially as he would be in a position to take an active hand in affairs were any shore raid contemplated by Howard.

Blake's appearance on deck the next morning was greeted by a yell and a volley of abuse from the *Marshall*; while, closer at hand, the consternation of Cutlip Sullivan was evident on the discovery of Blake's new position.

It was not so with Keough and young Boston, however; they were plainly glad to see Blake again, and Big Frank expressed decided satisfaction when Howard assigned Blake in charge of the diving pumps. The *Foster* had two excellent diving suits.

Promptly after breakfast the pumps were manned and Keough went down again. A man from the rival ship was also down, but as the *Marshall*'s pumps were rigged on the opposite side of the forecastle from the *Foster*, Blake could not make out the identity of the diver. This was not long in doubt, however.

After twenty minutes below Keough came up, his copper helmet was unscrewed, and he reported that the *Marshall* was anchored squarely over the stern portion of the wreck. The *Foster* lay twenty fathoms too far up to work on the stern, which hung on a crag of reef in shallow water, but lay over the bows where they had been found on the previous day.

"We want to rummage in the stern, not the bows, you lunkhead!" raved Howard furiously. "Get below again! Ain't you man enough to hold up your end with anybody Marshall can send down? You're big enough to eat old Steelfist himself!"

"Well, it *is* Steelfist!" growled Keough surlily, displaying a long scratch on his rubber sleeve. "I laid over to him, an' he come at me with his knife. I come up to git one for myself."

"Why in thunder didn't you say so? You come up like a dumb fool an' peel off palaver about bows an' sterns — want me to go down myself? What the —"

"Oh, shut yer head!" snapped Keough, in a rage. "Gimme a knife an' I'll git the son of a dogfish myself. What you s'pose I shipped in yer stinkin' old barge fer?"

Provided with a long knife from the galley, Keough turned to Blake.

"Give us plenty o' rope, Dude, an' keep them rats pumpin' steady, will you? I'm a-goin' to draw blood this time."

The helmet was screwed on, and Keough vanished. For five minutes Blake watched the line run out, then came a signal for less air.

Howard was himself tending the lines, and reported a moment

later that all was steady. Only the ceaseless grind of the pumps was heard, as all hands watched the water, fascinated.

"Gawd a'mighty!" burst from Howard. "Look at that'"

Between the two ships had risen a sudden seething whirl of water, followed by a burst of air-bubbles. A furious tug wrenched the lines from Howard's fingers, then came more bubbles bursting into froth on the surface.

"Pull, you fools!" yelled Blake sharply, seizing the lines.

Howard aided him, white-faced. Three, four, six fathoms of slack came in, then came a curled snarl — and the end of both lines, slashed off sharp.

As Blake realized what must have happened, a hail sounded from the other ship, and Steelfist Marshall appeared at her rail, his black mop of hair emerging from his diving suit.

"Send down another one tomorrow!" came the savage taunt. "Send the Dude, an' Boston, an' Sullivan, blast ye! Send yer whole blasted crew, Howard, an' come yerself!"

And with a laugh Steelfist vanished from sight.

Blake shuddered, and turned away. There was no use sending another man for Keough, even had another been willing to go. Big Frank was dead — had died when those bubbles came frothing to the surface, for these diving suits had no emergency valves.

Howard sprang to the rail, revolver in had, but no one was in sight aboard the *Marshall*. Then the maddened skipper began to curse, until even his waterfront sweepings shivered at the torrent of blasphemy that poured from him.

With hand aloft, Howard called heaven to witness his vow of revenge — a vow that included the *C. H. Marshall* and every soul aboard her.

From the *Marshall*'s decks volleyed a chorus of ribald merriment that ate into Howard's soul like acid into soft iron.

"Laugh, you condemned cut-throats!" he screamed. "Laugh yer fill! Ye'll laugh in hell tonight!"

Turning and leaping to the deck, his face like that of a madman, Howard roared out furious commands, and the men sprang to obedience.

Blake was puzzled. All diving was given up for the day, it seemed; the spare suit was taken to Howard's cabin and the skipper rushed after it, summoning Jackson and bidding Blake take the deck.

And in the cabin the two officers remained for the rest of the day, while the *Marshall*'s diving operations proceeded unhindered.

It was the general consensus of opinion among the men, however, that Howard had "something up his sleeve," and many were the conjectures voiced as to its nature. At four bells in the afternoon watch Jackson appeared, shook his head in response to Blake's question, and called away a boat's crew.

Jackson's business, it appeared, was to carry a kedge to a point opposite the *Marshall*, planting it firmly in the coral of the reef. When he returned, he flung an evil grin at Blake.

"Well haul off a ways tonight, Dude. Trust the Ol' Man to hand Steelfist one!"

He vanished again, this time taking a bucket of tar with him. An hour later Blake was sitting on the knighthead, alone with his pipe, when young Boston approached him somewhat diffidently.

"I'd like to ask ye somethin', Dude — sir, I mean."

Blake chuckled inwardly at this unwonted form of address, and eyed the speaker. As his nickname indicated, Boston was a callow youth, patently on his first voyage.

"Fire away, Boston. What's up?"

"I dunno, sir," and Boston shifted uneasily, with furtive glances aft. "I know you ain't Marshall's kind o' man, nor Howard's neither — and — and —"

"Out with it, old fellow," smiled Blake quietly. "You're quite right so far, and you can trust me. What's on your mind?"

"It's these here blamed murders!" broke out Boston, desperately. "I can't stand it, and I ain't goin' to stand it! I ain't any pirate an' murderer, Dude — I wish to Hades I'd never come to sea, I do!"

"So do I," nodded Blake grimly, his gray eyes narrowed. "Any more of the men feel that way about it, Boston?"

"I guess they do. We ain't seen no buried treasure, an' if we don't get out o' here that shark-hearted Marshall is goin' to get us all. If I talk to some o' the boys will you come ashore with us an' skip ship?"

The young fellow was in deathly earnest, else he never would have broached such an idea, as Blake knew.

"Yes," and Blake extended his hand. "Here's my fist on it, Boston. You and any of the other men who'll play square will find me willing to help. But mind, I'll have no funny work! It you come ashore with me, you'll obey me."

"Gawd knows, sir, all I want's to get out o' here!" and with that Boston shuffled away.

The two officers did not reappear until the wizened Chinese steward was serving the evening meal. It was then dead low water, and the fast-falling tropic evening had already cast a dusky screen over the lagoon.

"Now, my bullies," said the skipper softly, "we'll even up scores with Steelfist. We owe him two dead men already."

A low growl of assent arose from the men, but as yet Blake could see no signs of the indicated revenge. Howard proceeded to climb into the spare diving suit, to the breast of which had been fastened an electric torch incased in a tarry waterproof sheath.

"You tend the pumps, Mr. Blake," he grunted. "Mr. Jackson, you got that stuff tested?"

"It's workin' fine, sir," rejoined Jackson, his whine tinged with eagerness.

At this moment came a hail from the *Marshall* in the voice of her skipper.

"Hey, there, Howard! You waked up yet?"

"You'll know soon enough!" roared Howard, with a curse.

"Thanks for your good wishes," sneered Marshall. "We've been workin' this afternoon, and there ain't any stuff in that blasted wreck. If you're willin' to combine forces —"

"You go plumb to Hades!" bellowed Howard, shaking his fist at the darkness. "I wouldn't belive your word on a million Bibles, Steelfist Charley! I wouldn't touch ye if you was drownin' to death! I hope I see ye roastin' on the devil's gridiron an' beggin' yer heart out fer water!"

Trembling with rage, Howard signed to Blake to screw on his helmet. No further word came from the other ship.

There was a heavy splash alongside the gangway, and Blake looked up to see that Jackson had flung something overboard and seemed to be watching it. Howard, completely incased from head to foot, was assisted down.

At the foot of the ladder he halted, gripped something carefully, and was lowered away out of sight.

Wondering mightily what all this secrecy was about, Blake assured himself that the pumps were working steadily, and then approached the main rigging where Jackson stood.

"Keep away from them wires, fer Gawd's sake!" broke out the mate in a hoarse whisper.

Blake halted abruptly.

"Wires?" he repeated. "What —"

"Get back to them pumps, will ye? Don't foul them batteries under the poop, or we'll all blow to bloomin' Hades together. It's hard enough without payin' out these blasted wires in the dark —"

Blake turned and went back to the pumps. He felt suddenly stunned, horrified beyond words, heartsick.

Jackson was paying out wire, and batteries were placed under the poop! And what was the heavy object which had been dropped over the side and which Howard had caught up so tenderly as he went into the depths?

Taking up the lines, Blake paid them out slowly, a premonition of horror upon him which he could not shake off.

Behind him were grouped the men, tense, expectant, silent. Through the quivering hush of the tropic night came a mutter of talk from the other ship, the scratch of a match, the snatch of a chanty in Paddy Ryan's voice —

The lines ceased to pay out, and Howard signaled for more air. Cutlip and young Boston were at the pumps, and Blake, who seldom swore, mouthed an oath as he turned and sped up the grinding wheels.

A moment later he felt the haul-in jerks.

"Bear a hand here, two of you!" he snapped hoarsely.

The dripping coils wound up beside him. Howard, who had gone to six fathoms, paused halfway up to relieve the blood pressure; that two minutes of waiting seemed an age to Blake.

At last the huge helmet broke water, and Howard was hauled aboard. At the same instant Jackson barked out a curt order.

"Port watch for'ard! Lay on to that capstan, and sharp about it!"

Evidently it mattered nothing that the *Marshall* would hear the clinking pawls. But, as the men fell to work, Jackson halted them abruptly.

From the *Marshall* came the clatter of oars, voices, and the deep "Give way!" of Steelfist himself as a boat set out for shore.

"Hell and blazes!" swore Howard, floundering ponderously in his clumsy leaded boots. "Get me out o' this rig! Eight o' you bullies tumble into the cutter — jump, you rats! You stay aboard, Blake."

With laborious rapidity the dripping suit was flung aside. The skipper dashed below, returning with a .45 in either hand, and promptly leaped down to the boat.

"Shove off, bullies!" Howard turned and flung a low order over his shoulder. "Soon's you're kedged out, Jackson, touch her off! Send the Dude with all the men but you an' a couple more — we'll need help ashore —"

The big cutter gathered way and was lost in the darkness. Now under Jackson's curses the windlass began its song and the *Foster* moved slowly away from Marshall, kedged out toward the reef.

Blake seized the opportunity and leaped for the after cabins. He had lost the revolver gained from Bully Forrester, but in Bingham's cabin he found another and a box of cartridges. Shoving them into his pocket, he regained the deck to hear Jackson bawling for him.

"Dude! Git into that boat — where the hell are ye?"

"Coming!" sang out Blake.

"Hustle your rats! Over with you!"

Blake dropped into the boat, hearing the whine of young Boston at his elbow. Above them stood the figure of Jackson, a black blur in the main rigging.

"Give way, you fools!" cried Jackson, his voice shrill with excitement. "Give way! Give way! Now laugh, Steelfist, curse you!"

And, as the boat shoved off, there came a low, muffled roar. The *Marshall*'s tall masts and rigging quivered against a red flame; her whole structure seemed to plunge on end like a sounding whale; the roar burst into a racking explosion that sent Blake down amid his shrieking men as the boat rocked and reeled.

Howard had exacted a terrible vengeance!

CHAPTER XIV

SWITCHING COMMANDERS

Darkness intense and terrible — and the screams of men.

Came shots and yells from the beach, with Howard's deep bellow calling on Blake to hurry. In the starlight Blake saw the masts of the *Marshall* projecting from the water, as his men began to pull mechanically.

But after the first horrible awe and realization, there came swift reaction. Hardened as these men were, wholesale murder was far from their hearts. The bowman suddenly gasped, then flung his oar across the gunwales and broke into a screaming sob.

"Gawd's vengeance on the cursed job! There's a floater — let them murderers ashore fight it out — I'm done, I am!"

A rough chorus of approval heaved up, and the men stopped rowing. Young Boston began to pray. Some one struck him down with an oath.

"That ain't no floater — he's alive!" cried Sullivan.

The body which had struck the bowman's oar swirled in between the halted blades and reached for the gunwale.

Blake leaped forward and helped draw the man inboard. As he fell over the thwarts, sobbing something, an exclamation broke from the men.

"It's Ole! It's the Finn!"

Blake helped the man sit up. Ole seemed quite unhurt, and gazed into his face with sobbing recognition.

"Who went ashore?" demanded Blake sharply. "Speak quick, now!"

The old fear of authority fell upon Ole, and he shivered.

"All but me an' de mate an' t'ree more, sir. Ay —"

A long and furious bellow rose from Howard, followed by two more shots and a chorus of yells. Evidently there was a desperate battle going forward. Young Boston suddenly rose with a shrill cry.

"Dude, we ain't goin' to help them pirates! You take us out o' here an' we'll stick to ye, won't we lads?"

"Sure thing!" rumbled a hearty response. "Say the word, Dude. We're all with ye, sir!"

"Der bo'sun," spoke up Ole Kafban, "an' Paddy Ryan an' mabbe odders is full oop o' fightin', Dude. I come too if ju help Miss Pebbody."

Here was the crucial instant, and Blake seized it.

"Men, will you stand by to help Miss Peabody. Say aye, and we'll beat these murdering ruffians at their own game."

"Aye!" growled the men.

"Good. Give way!"

The oars dipped, and Blake turned the boat toward the northern headland, running parallel with the beach. The two crews were still engaged in furious battle, Marshall cursing his men and Howard cursing everyone impartially; by the sounds, the fight was setting toward the southern headland.

Blake, suddenly finding himself in command of ten men, was no less swift in grasping his best plan of campaign. From Marshall's attempted parley earlier in the evening, he comprehended that nothing had been found in the sunken wreck; this would indicate that Marshall had taken his crew ashore to make a thorough raid of the island.

First, therefore, thought Blake, he must reach the bungalow and communicate with Wicliff. Then to capture the almost undefended Foster, get what recruits he could from Steelfist's crew, and the two skippers would be forced to come to terms.

With the *Marshall* blown up and the *Foster* in his own hands, the game was won, it seemed.

Bidding the men wait, Blake leaped ashore as the bow grounded. He ran up the path to the bungalow, calling out Wicliff's name as he went, but there was no answer. To his surprise and dismay, he reached the bungalow to find it deserted as before, but this time there were clearly no natives in the bush.

Striking a light, he found that the bungalow held no weapons at all, and so went back toward the boat, cogitating. This un-looked for desertion meant a change of plan.

"All right, men," he called softly, reaching the beach. "Ole, you lay ashore here with me. Young Boston, if I give you a gun can you capture the *Foster* and hold her?"

A hearty growl of assent went up from the men. Blake handed over his revolver to Boston when the voice of Sullivan reached him.

"I kin get some o' them Marshall bullies to jine us, Dude! Say the word, an' I'll lay up along the beach till I see the bo'sun or Ryan."

Blake reposed no confidence in Sullivan; yet, if the man wanted to join Howard, it was best to let him go. If, on the other hand, he kept his word, so much the better.

"Hop along with you, then," said Blake, and Cutlip promptly splashed away and vanished. "Now, Boston, you get the *Foster* and hang on to her, see? You can hold off any boat-attack. Ole and I will hold the bungalow, with any recruits we can get from the *Marshall*'s crew. I'll get in touch with the natives tomorrow, and we'll take these murdering skippers back to 'Frisco in irons. Give way!"

With a hearty mutter of encouragement, the men dipped their oars, and were gone.

Sullivan had slipped into the lantanas and vanished. With the Finn waiting patiently, Blake stood in silence for a moment, considering.

All sounds of conflict had died away along the beach. What had become of Bully Forrester and the other men blown up with the *Mar-*

shall, Blake neither knew nor cared; he was more anxious about the outcome of the fracas between the skippers.

"Come along, Ole," he said at length. "We'll investigate our friends yonder."

With the Finn at his heels, he struck into the bush and started down toward the south headland, cautiously enough. Snaky lianas brushed his face like ghostly fingers, palmettos squeaked and rustled as they chafed together; from the shore came the slap-slap of waves, but there was no sound of the presence of men.

At an opening in the bush, Blake found himself opposite the dim bulk of the ship; the moon was just dipping over the horizon. With a word of caution to Ole, Blake crept to the edge of the lantanas and peered out.

Just below him, at the lip of the tide, two empty boats rose and fell gently. Advance farther, he dare not.

With a suddenness that hurt, Jackson's voice drifted over the lagoon, followed instantly by a little burst of shots and a wild yell. Once more the mate's voice rose but this time in a long scream that was cut short.

Blake caught his breath sharply — the *Foster* had been taken, and Jackson had there met his end.

"What the devil is that slimy Dude up to!" rang out a deep voice twenty feet away, and Howard loomed against the sky, cursing.

Marshall's grating laugh swept up.

"Look's like a hurrah's nest, Howard —"

"Curse you, is this some o' your work?" snarled Howard. Steelfist remained invisible to Blake, but other forms of men blotted out the stars.

"Cut out the cursing, you hoary old fool!" exclaimed Steelfist. "The Dude's euchred you, blast him — this ain't no time for us to be fighting! Get busy, now. You blew my ship up, and you've lost your own. It's the Dude against both of us, and we've got to pull together."

"And you cut in on the loot, eh?" grated Howard in fury. "Passage home for you — that's all! You're licked, Steelfist, licked good!"

"Oh, are you sure of that?" Marshall laughed again. "How about my mate, Bower, eh? He an' his men are scouring the island for the girl an' the Gospel-shark, an' they ought to get here pretty quick. Bower's got the rifles, too."

At this information, Blake stiffened where he crouched.

"You're a handy liar, Steelfist," returned Howard, but there was doubt in his voice, "I got you licked right here —"

"If you think so, start scrappin' again!" taunted Marshall. "There's no loot unless I share fifty-fifty, see? Where d'ye think you'll find it?"

"What d'ye mean?" demanded Howard, "What's your foxy trick now?"

"It takes no trick to know that anything what was ever in that old wreck ain't there now, you fool! Didn't I tell you that this evening? The old hymn-singer's got it, blast him! If Bower don't round him up, we'll go through his house. Fifty-fifty — speak up quick!"

Howard stood silent for a moment. No sound came from the *Foster*.

"I don't trust you any more'n I would a rattler," said Howard grudgingly. "But I guess you're right. We'll split even. If we don't find nothing — you stop here, savvy? And I'm in command."

"Take you," snapped Marshall with a chuckle. "Tell what's left of your rats to hustle over here, an' give us a lead yourself."

Blake turned swiftly and caught the Finn's shoulder.

"Ole, you stay around and watch those fellows. If you get a chance, cut out the bo'sun, Paddy Ryan, or any one else you can trust, and bring 'em to the house. I'm going back there. Understand?"

"Ay got ju, Dude," nodded Ole confidently, and Blake crawled away hurriedly. From the condition of the bungalow he knew that Long Rube's party could not have come that way. Therefore Bower, who must have been sent ashore shortly after dark and in absolute silence, had probably landed at the south headland and had begun to sweep the island from that direction. His whereabouts was now a mystery.

Since no sound of shots had lifted from across the island, Blake felt convinced that Wicliff was still keeping the natives out of a fight, though probably aware of Bower's presence.

Gaining the bungalow, he found it as before — deserted, more silent than the silent night outside. But as he stepped heavily to the veranda and felt for a match there came the slightest of rustles, the sound of a sharply caught breath — and again silence.

Blake stood stock still, his mind leaping to Bower. Was an ambush planted here? Had Long Rube's party circled the island? He cursed his own ignorance of that expedition, which had caused him to give his revolver to Boston.

He could descry nothing in the pitch-blackness of the room before him. Lips clenched, he took a step forward — *"click!"* A weapon had cocked, somewhere.

"Hold up, Bower!" he exclaimed sharply. "This is Blake — I've taken the *John Foster*, and now we'll talk terms."

For an instant longer there was tense silence. Then —

"Oh, thank God!" breathed a voice, and something brushed into his arms. "I — I was afraid —"

"Mary Peabody, by the Lord Harry!" he ejaculated softly, holding the slight figure to him. "Why, girl — where did you come from? Here, come out on the veranda and tell me about it. Where's Wicliff?"

Despite her half-hysterical laugh of protest, he lifted and carried her to one of the Singapore chairs. Then he took the cocked revolver from her hand and carefully lowered the hammer.

Her fingers clung to him for a moment and loosened.

"I've been at the village," she said, forcing quiet into her voice. "Mr. Wicliff was gone with the men — I don't know where. One of the women ran in with word that strange men were coming, and — and I ran this way. I had just got in the house when I heard you coming —"

"And here I am," smiled Blake. "Did the women scatter?"

"Yes — they had some place to hide, but I was too frightened to do anything but come here. Silly, I know —"

"Not at all," said Blake quietly. "The point is, that this is no place for you to stay. Here's the situation —"

He told what had happened on that eventful day, sparing nothing, and questioned her in turn. Under the spell of his steady, even voice she quickly regained her own poise, and when her hand touched his arm again he found it without a tremor, while her own voice became cool.

When the *Marshall* was blown up Wicliff had been at the village with the men. At the explosion they had started off into the bush, and had not been seen since. The party under Bower had arrived unexpectedly, and apparently without molestation from Wicliff.

"Then," said Blake, "the best thing you can do is to go up to that hut where I was hidden yesterday — do you know the place?"

"I know it. You think Marshall and Howard are coming here?"

"Most certainly. I —"

Blake whirled at a crackle from the path.

The moonlight was filtering into the clearing by this time, and at the entrance of the trail to the beach he caught sight of a dark figure. He lifted the revolver, but as he cocked it, the figure cried out quickly.

"Don't shood! Vos dot you, Dude?"

Blake recognized the Dutchman's voice.

"That you, Dutch? Step for'ard here, and quick about it! Who's with you?"

The Dutchman advanced and showed himself to be alone.

"I met dot man Ole," he panted. "I vant to pay Marshall for some liddle t'ings, I'm vit' you, Dude! Ole, he's comin'."

Another figure crashed forward, joining the Dutchman. Blake lowered his weapon with a breath of relief.

"Come along, Ole — both of you. Miss Peabody's here."

The girl stepped to his side, and the two men stood before them, staring and grinning sheepishly.

"Mr. Blake has told me all about you, Ole," said the girl softly. "I want to thank you for sticking up for me — you're a good man, and I'm glad to call you my friend."

The old Peabody blood stirring within her; the girl said neither too much nor too little — just just enough to send the Finn into a glow.

"Ay go hell fer ju, Miss Pebbody," he returned, with earnest embarrassment and his hulking figure straightened a little. "Ay go hell for save ju!"

And none of those who heard him knew how he was to make good that word before the night was out.

"We've no time to spare, Miss Peabody," and Blake turned. "Take Ole, please, and go up to that grass hut at once. No matter what happens, you stay there! Ole, I'll trust you to take care of Miss Peabody — go at once, please!"

She put out her hand to him, and for a long moment his eyes held hers in the semi-darkness.

"Thank you, Mr. Blake. Good night!"

A moment later she was lost in the gloom of the bush, and the Finn with her. The Dutchman stood uneasily, waiting.

Blake looked down at the lagoon, now resplendent with the moonlight; every tiny wavelet bursting over the reef was tipped with silver, while the *John Foster* lay tall and silent, a fairy toy of shimmering light and shadow, outlined in silvery light from rippling waterline to the frayed dogvanes at her soaring trucks.

From where Blake stood the line of curving beach was invisible.

"Got any matches, Dutch?" asked Blake, turning. "Good — then rummage around the house here and get some kind of weapon. I'm going down the path and see what's doing. You've heard nothing of Bower's party?"

The Dutchman shook his head, and Blake strode down the path that led to the beach. He was not yet in sight of the circling sands when he halted abruptly at the low growl of voices ahead. Purposely, he snapped a twig, his revolver ready.

"Who's there?" sang out a voice.

Once more Blake breathed relief.

"It's Blake, bo'sun! Marshall with you?"

"Divil a bit," returned the tones of Paddy Ryan, jubilantly. "We're with ye, Dude, me lad! Me an' Fancy Harry an' the Bottle Heaver an' two more — we're with ye, matey, an' we've skipped that murderin' Steelfist fer good."

A shadowy group of figures filed into view on the path ahead, then the voice of the bo'sun came to Blake anew.

"It's lucky for this here Sullivan ye spoke up prompt, Dude! We had a notion the frowsy dog was misleadin' us with his lies, an' my knife was ready for him. But all's well, mate — excepting that Marshall an' Howard an' their gang are comin' hell-bent for election, right behind."

"How close?" queried Blake, meeting the dark figures and shaking hands all around, even including Sullivan in his delighted greeting, for he was overjoyed that the man had played fair.

"We cut out o' the bunch when they was starting an' run ahead," explained Ryan. "Got any guns?"

"One for myself — come along," and Blake turned. "If we can lick that gang before Long Rube shows up, we're all right."

CHAPTER XV

WHERE THE TREASURE WAS

Seven men at his back, the clearing flooded with moonlight, the path beyond obscured and dark — Blake made his dispositions quickly.

He posted the men at the edges of the clearing, in a circle, and ordered them to show themselves only at the bo'sun's whistle. Fancy Harry he retained on the bungalow veranda, and the two men lighted their pipes for a short smoke.

"How many men with Bower, bo'sun?"

"Six, Dude. They got all the rifles. We had a devil of a scrap out on the beach, after that condemned Howard blew up the *Marshall*! Besides us, there's only eight left, an' the two skippers. Was that you took the *Foster*?"

"Young Boston," explained Blake. He began to narrate what had happened, when a low warning hail from Paddy Ryan cut him short.

"I hear the skipper cussin', Dude!"

Blake and Lovell knocked out their pipes and waited, tense.

A moment later the sounds of men crashing through the bush became clear — seamen are not made for such work. The opening of the path blurred and darkened with grouping figures, which did not venture into the light of the clearing.

For a long minute no sound broke the silence — Blake's men kept quiet, the attackers were evidently reconnoitering. Then two huge shapes moved out into the moonlight, and Blake saw Howard and Steelfist Marshall side by side.

In each skipper's hand was a revolver, and Howard's was an automatic. Blake noted that fact swiftly.

"No one here," spat out Marshall "Come on, boys!"

Blake moved forward to the steps, where he was still in shadow.

"That's far enough, Steelfist," he ordered quietly. "I've got you covered, and my men are all around you. I've got the *Foster*, too. Want to make terms?"

"No, you cursed liar!" roared Howard. "Come on, boys!"

"Stop or drop!" cried Blake grimly.

The only answer was a yell from Marshall, and the group of figures dashed forward. Steelfist's revolver spat fire — and as it did so, Blake threw down on Howard's massive bulk and pulled trigger.

"All right, bo'sun!"

Lovell's whistle shrilled out. Howard fell with a single gasping curse, and Marshall tripped over him.

Before Steelfist could gain his feet Blake's men raised a wild shout and charged, the Dutchman leaping in first of all on Marshall himself, and knocking away the latter's revolver.

One of Howard's men knifed the Dutchman twice, in the back. Blake shot the man dead — and up staggered Steelfist Marshall, spitting blood and curses, lashing into the thick of the fight.

Blake thrust his revolver away and bored in. He reached Marshall just as the deadly steel hand knocked Lovell sprawling, and staggered the skipper with a straight punch to the jaw. Marshall whirled, Blake drove his fist home again, and the skipper reeled back.

The fight was over, however. Panic-stricken by the ring of men leaping out on them from the darkness, the attackers broke blindly for the shore and Marshall, though wild with fury, smashed his way after them and was gone, still roaring curses.

Blake was content to let him go, and called in the men from any pursuit.

Picking up Howard's automatic, he found the clip full, and passed his own half-empty weapon to Ryan. The revolver knocked away from Marshall he handed to Fancy Harry, and then proceeded to take stock of damages.

Though short, the battle had been sickeningly bloody.

The Dutchman was dead, knifed twice to the heart; the Bottle Heaver lay inert, a boat-stretcher resting on his skull. One of the attacking seamen had been shot by Blake, while Sullivan returned with a ferocious oath and exhibited a bloody knife which had accounted for another in the pursuit.

Howard, the first victim, was the only one who still lived. He was shot through the chest, and was quite conscious but unable to speak; his glittering, pig-like eyes gleamed up at the surrounding men so venomously that Blake shivered in disgust, and Paddy Ryan crossed himself furtively.

"Carry him into the house, two of you," commanded Blake. "Bo'sun, you'd better lay down to the shore-end of that path and give us warning of any further attack — but I don't think there'll be any. Paddy, you come with me; the rest of you keep a sharp lookout, for Bower's gang isn't very far off and those shots will draw him. I'll be back soon enough."

Howard was as helpless to move as to speak, and once laid down inside Blake saw that his wound was a fatal one — the man's tremendous vitality alone held life in him. With a nod to Ryan, Blake left the house and strode off up the path that led to the grass hut.

It never occurred to him that he had virtually left Cutlip Sullivan in charge of the bungalow.

With Ryan at his elbow, he quickly climbed the path to the hut. Ole was keeping good guard and challenged him at the edge of the banana grove. Leaving Paddy Ryan with the Finn, Blake passed on toward the hut and found Mary Peabody waiting, anxious-eyed.

"What's happened?" she queried.

"Nothing particularly," laughed Blake. "Marshall and Howard

tried to bump us, and we scared them off with a few shots. Everything all right up here? Any sign of Wicliff?"

His strong face was very quiet and composed in the soft moonlight, which struck the grimness out of it; but the moonlight could not banish the look that had come into his eyes, at the sight of her.

"Yes, all's well here," replied the girl, a tinge of color creeping into her face. Yet she met his eyes steadily. "Was any one hurt? We've seen no one here."

"We hurt Captain Howard," said Blake, glossing over the details. "Let's have a look at those fellows — that's one reason I came up here."

Although the house was hidden, from the hut they had a clean sweep of the lagoon and its curving half-moon of beach, now flooded with moonlight.

By the two boats on the shore was clustered a group of men — Marshall and his followers. Farther down, toward the southern headland, Blake made out a third boat, and realized that it must have been that used by Bower. Therefore, his theory had been correct.

"What's that?" The girl gripped his arm suddenly.

Blake turned to where the *Foster* lay limned in black against the silvern sea beyond. From the ship was drifting a swinging, rousing chorus, hoarse-throated as if given tongue by men who had drunk too well — the old hauling-chanty that was sung when Bluff King Hal ruled Merrie England.

> *"Oh, haul the bowline, Katy is my darling,*
> *Oh, haul the bowline, the bowline* haul!
>
> *"Oh, haul the bowline, London girls are towing,*
> *Oh, haul the bowline, the bowline* haul!
>
> *"Oh, haul the bowline, the packet is a-rolling,*
> *Oh, haul the bowline, the bowline* haul!"

Blake grunted, his gray eyes narrowed.

"H-m! They've broken into Howard's locker, evidently. Hello! — Looks as though Marshall were up to tricks!"

The group by the two boats had suddenly leaped into activity, for that chanty must have carried to Steelfist, who could easily guess the cause thereof.

Watching with growing anxiety, Blake saw the men run out both boats and leap in. It seemed that Marshall was about to make a bold stroke for the *John Foster*, but if so that stroke was halted almost as it began.

Spats of fire broke from the *Foster*'s rail, and the lagoon echoed to the crack of rifles. Beyond a doubt young Boston's men were drunk, for they poured a hail of lead toward the two boats, firing as fast as they could pull trigger.

Nonetheless, they must have made things altogether too warm for Marshall. The bowman in one of the boats crumpled up, another man screamed out shrilly, and the boats foamed back to shore hastily.

"Good for Boston!" laughed Blake, as the firing ceased. "Drunk or not, they have rifles and won't allow Steelfist Marshall within hailing distance. Confound it, I wish we had those guns!"

The situation did not lack a certain element of rough humor, for, realizing that they had effectually repulsed Marshall, young Boston's crew roared out an adaptation which must have stung Steelfist to the quick:

> *"As I was a-walking down Paradise Street,*
> *Good-by, fare-ye-well! Good-by, fare-ye-well!*
> *Ol' Steelfist Marshall I chanct for to meet —*
> *Hurray, my boys, we're outward bound!*
>
> *"Says he, I've lost my ship an' crew,*
> *Good-by, fare-ye-well! Good-by, fare-ye-well!*
> *The Dude has lammed me black an' blue —*
> *Hurray, my boys, we're outward bound!"*

There was more of it, but of such a nature that Blake turned hastily, his face very red, and led the girl outside into the moonlight, over the lip of the crest.

"There's no danger of their sailing away?" asked the girl quietly.

"Hardly! They could kedge or tow out, and couldn't navigate when they got out. No, the *Foster* is safe enough. All that worries me is Long Rube Bower and his sweet gang of cutthroats. And where can Wicliff be? By the way, Marshall's presence ashore, as I told you, is due to the fact that he found the wreck empty of treasure. Has Wicliff ever mentioned it to you?"

For a moment she looked up at him, then smiled.

"Yes, Mr. Blake —"

"You mean Jack," and Blake smiled in turn. "Mary's ever so much more suitable than Miss Peabody — so go on about the treasure."

"Yes, Jack," she nodded, her eyes twinkling. "He spoke about it to me when I first came ashore. He had recovered the money years ago, and several times wrote to find any of my grandfather's heirs who might be alive. As we never got the letters, however, he never got any answer; so he put the money into a chest in the bungalow —"

"What!" exclaimed Blake sharply. "It's there in plain sight?"

"No, hardly! The chest is in the little cellar — just a hole reached by a trap in the dining room floor. Mr. Wicliff showed me the money the day before I went to the village — what's the matter?"

For Blake had turned abruptly, his eyes hard.

"I'd better get back to the house in a hurry," he rejoined. "Those fellows will be prowling around, and if they light on that treasure it's all up."

"Give the money to Captain Marshall, if he'll only —" began the girl.

"Nothing doing, Mary," snapped Blake, then laughed. "Knuckle down to that tough? I should say not! We're going to beat him, Mary Peabody — beat him at his own specialty, and then send you home with that money in your pocket. Now, take good care of yourself, and whatever you do, stay here. Good night for the present!"

"Good night, Jack!" she said softly.

But Blake was not destined to return to the bungalow so speedily as he wished. As he rejoined his two men Ryan plucked at his arm, and drew him on to the edge of the bluff, over the northern headland.

"Will ye be lookin' at that, Dude!"

Under the brilliant three-quarters moon the lagoon was as light as day. The wreck of the *Marshall* was indicated by her rigging, still above the water, for she lay in but six fathoms. A boat was just putting out from the *Foster* with ribald shouts.

"What'll be them dots in the old Marshall's fore-rigging, Dude?"

Blake made out three figures, evidently men.

"Ole wasn't the only one to escape, Paddy — I hope to Heaven Boston won't murder them!"

Paddy Ryan, to judge by his muttered curse, evidently did not second the wish.

It soon proved that young Boston had no murderous intents, however, despite his Dutch courage. The boat halted under the fore rigging of the *Marshall*, and one by one the three figures climbed down. A jubilant yell, the oars flashed silver, and the boat headed back for the *Foster*.

"Here, Paddy," exclaimed Blake, satisfied, "I've got to get back to the bungalow. You follow this path," and he pointed out the trail which led from the crest through the banana groves to the village, "and see if you can't meet up with some of those natives. Long Rube's party ought to come from that direction. If you meet 'em, join in with the crowd unless you can get away; but see to it that I get warning, and that they keep away from the hut up here. Understand?"

Ryan nodded, wrinkling up his face anxiously, as well he might. There was no danger that Bower knew of his desertion, but the duty was none to his liking.

"I'll do me best, sir — what the divil's that?"

"Dude!" the voice of Fancy Harry rang out from below. "Hey, Dude! Git here in a hurry!"

There was a note of desperation in the tones that sent Blake plunging off down the path, wondering if by any chance the men could have found that chest of money. But they had found worse than money.

Blake reached the clearing to see the house blazing with light, while another cry from Fancy Harry ended with startling abruptness. It was followed instantly by the voice of Cutlip Sullivan.

"Urrk-uh-uh-uh-urrk! I'm Cutlip Sullivan, and I eats 'em alive — whooey!"

Darting to the door, Blake was in time to see the bo'sun reel across the room, crash into the opposite wall, and fall limply. Then he stared aghast at the scene which met his eyes.

CHAPTER XVI
TORTURE

The bo'sun lay inert, while Sullivan stood over him, stretcher in hand, and flapped his arms grotesquely.

The Bottle Heaver and the remaining two men were stretched out on the floor half drunk; between them stood Wicliff's big sandalwood chest, smashed open. From this had been taken a brandy case, also smashed to flinders, and empty bottles rolled on the floor.

How long this silent orgy had been going on before Fancy Harry discovered it, there was no saying.

Head and shoulders resting against the wall, was the body of Howard, with Cutlip Sullivan's knife-haft protruding from his neck.

As Blake stared in horrified incredulity Sullivan turned and saw him. A torrent of blasphemy poured from the seaman's throat; swinging up his boat-stretcher, Sullivan leaped across the room with a roar, murder in his face. The other three seamen looked up in stupid, drunken mirth.

Blake sprang in, dodged the deadly sweep of the stretcher and swung to Sullivan's jaw with all his weight and fury behind the blow. The "cock of the fo'c's'le" threw out his arms and went down as if shot.

Catching up one of the rolling bottles, Blake crossed to the senseless form of the bo'sun, turned it over, and poured brandy into the man's mouth. It was all too plain that Wicliff had kept the stuff in the chest along with other medicines, and that the men had broken into it the first thing.

Being unhurt except for a crack over the head, Fancy Harry sat up and cursed for more brandy. Then he looked into Blake's ice-cold eyes and scrambled to his feet.

"The fools!" he cried, kicking the prostrate Bottle Heaver.

"You get back to your post," said Blake coldly. "I've got to get these fellows in shape to fight before Long Rube shows up. Skip along now!"

The bo'sun turned and vanished. Leaving the murderer, Sullivan, where he lay, Blake seized on the other three seamen. He was in a cold rage at their criminal negligence in not staying at least passably sober, and without compunction he began to awaken them in fo'c's'le fashion, using foot and fist and voice as he had seldom thought ever to use them.

One by one he shot the three out through the doorway, then jerked Sullivan to his feet. Quite knocked out by Blake's one blow, the man was now coming to himself, and reeled out to the veranda. Blake kicked him down to the moonlit clearing with the others.

"You're a fine bunch of swine, you are —" He was checked abruptly by a faint and apparently distant hail lifting above the trees, in the voice of Paddy Ryan.

"Look out, Dude! They're past me an' comin' — I'm off to get —"

"Dude!" came a roar from Lovell, down the beach path. "The skipper's sneakin' up on —"

As Blake leaped for the veranda, tugging out his revolver, he heard shots from the crest above — the crest where lay the grass hut, with Mary Peabody. The thicket of lantanas seemed suddenly to break out into voices of men.

"Get up here out of the light, you fools!" shouted Blake, at the half-stupefied men.

The Bottle Heaver and the others started to obey clumsily, but Cutlip Sullivan shook his fist in maudlin defiance.

"To hell wid ye, Dude — ye lop-eared —"

A rifle flashed out at the edge of the clearing, and Sullivan went down, coughing out his life.

Other rifles cracked; Blake heard the bullets ripping into the house all around him, and a wild yell in Marshall's voice answered by a burst of shouts from all sides. So, then, Bower had come!

"Use those bottles for weapons, men!" cried Blake, shoving the others inside. "Here they come —"

From the path across the clearing he saw Marshall's men breaking cover in a wild charge. When Marshall himself came into the moonlight Blake fired, and saw Steelfist go down.

Then men broke from the bush all around, surged on the veranda, and the darkness of the house was filled with a shrieking, cursing, sobbing riot of battle, where quarter was not asked or given.

Blake, knowing there was no escape, drew aside with a grim determination to make each of his shots tell. From six feet distant a revolver spat fire at him, and as the bullet nicked his ear, Blake caught the savage face of Long Rube Bower behind the gun.

He fired, saw the mate fall, and then was rushed back by knife-armed men. After that first volley, the rifles had been discarded.

In that moment the three remaining brandy-drinkers retrieved themselves nobly and well, swinging into the fray with knife and bottle — then the bellow of Steelfist Marshall rose anew, and Blake knew that the skipper was still unharmed.

Vainly he tried to get another shot at Steelfist; twice he shot down men who leaped at him, then a wild rush of bodies sent him to the floor and his revolver whirled out of his hand.

Blake came up, fighting like a demon, only to go down again, dazed, under the unseen blow of a stretcher. Before he could rise some one had leaped on him, a knee in his back, grinding him down and strangling him, and hearing the brutal laugh of Marshall above him, he felt himself tied hand and foot.

There was a shot, and the Bottle Heaver screamed. Then Steelfist's voice rang out again.

"Haul the Dude down to the beach, two o' you! I got use for him later. Lively, now! Where's Bower? Hey, Rube —"

As Blake was lifted and carried away, he could hear the skipper cursing like a madman over the mate's body, and smiled grimly to himself.

Five minutes later he was unceremoniously dumped in the sand near the two boats, and left to his own reflections. Finding that his lashings were too well tied to be loosened, Blake composed himself to await events.

He was under no illusions as to his present situation. Steelfist Marshall had not spared him through pity, but through cruelty, and doubtless had some savage reprisal in mind. But what of Paddy Ryan and the bo'sun?

Fancy Harry seemed to have completely vanished. From Ryan's one shout of warning, Blake gathered that the little Irishman had slipped through Bower's party and was now desperately scurrying in search of Wicliff and the natives. That hunt, he reflected, promised to be vain so far as he himself was concerned.

He knew that Marshall must now be going through the bungalow; a moment later a wild yell of triumph that shrilled through the mass of jungle apprised him that the search must have been successful.

Blake gave vent to an inward curse.

"I wouldn't care so much for myself," he thought bitterly, "but if that old ass Wicliff had only hidden the loot properly, it might still be saved from Steelfist. What about Ole, I wonder? Those first shots I heard —"

With unhappy surmise fast growing upon him, he was interrupted by the arrival of two men, both bearing knife-wounds, who cursed and kicked him impartially. Both reeked of brandy, and Blake knew that what was left of the stuff had found its mark.

Then from the direction of the bungalow lifted a chorus — the short, snappy chanty used in furling the bunt of the heavy sails.

> *"Way-hay-hay — my old woman's a divil for gin —*
> *We'll pay Paddy Doyle for his boot!"*

The reason for this was made clear a moment later. Down the beach came four men, each pair carrying the end of a long pole that disclosed itself as the rail of the bungalow veranda. In the center was slung a large chest, whose weight caused the four men to stagger.

Steelfist Marshall followed, a rifle in his hand. On closer approach, Blake saw a streak of blood on the skipper's cheek, which accounted for his first bullet. After him came the rest of the gang, singing and cursing and yelling.

Blake's first thought was that they had thoroughly looted the house, for they carried furniture, strips of rail, and in fact everything which could be moved or torn away. Then — Blake went sick as he looked.

For, marching between two men was a white figure which he knew instantly. It was Mary Peabody.

"Stow that chest in my boat!" snapped Marshall. "There's more of it, bullies, an' when we've got it we'll —"

He was interrupted by a chorus of the men.

"Let's have a look at it, cap'n! Slim Jack can open her up — he's picked more'n one lock in his time!"

"All right, then — make sure," nodded Marshall. "An' keep that girl away from the Dude, blast you!"

Mary Peabody was halted on the other side of the group, and Blake caught her eyes fastened on him. But there was no fear in her face — rather sorrow and pity, and a hopeless bewilderment that sickened him anew.

Slim Jack, a grinning waterfront rat, knelt before the chest and fumbled with its locks. There was a click; after a moment, another; then a third click, and with a maudlin laugh the seaman raised the creaking lid. Marshall shoved back the men and leaned forward, then —

"Sand!" he roared, straightening up with such fury in his face that the men shrank back from him. "Sand! Gawd —"

For a moment his rage choked him, and in the silence Blake's laugh rang out. So, then, Wicliff had not been such a fool after all.

"Pile up that stuff!" foamed Marshall, raving curses like a madman. "Pile up that stuff, you blasted rats — lively! Tie up that girl — do the job right, you Slim Jack, or by Heaven you die here an' now!"

Under his threatening rifle and more threatening manner, the men leaped to his word in wild panic. Unresisting, Mary Peabody allowed two of them to tie her feet together. As with Marshall, the exultation of the men had given way to bitter fury on discovering that their gold was but sand.

When he saw the girl seized, Jack Blake also went mad, and writhed in his bonds unavailingly, until Marshall's vicious curses turned to a terribly ominous laughter that was drowned in a sudden crackle of wood.

Not far from the boats, and close to the group, was that same tangled mass of driftwood which had hidden Foster's boat from Blake. It was now low tide, and the mass had washed up to high water mark.

One of the men had touched a match to the tangle, and over it the rest were now heaping the bungalow loot — chairs, veranda rails, smashed table, doors. As it began to flame up, Steelfist turned and his boot thudded into Blake's ribs.

"Now, my bucko, we'll have some talk out o' you! Want to taste that fire? Then loosen up! Where's the gold, huh?"

Realizing at last the meaning of that fire, Blake went cold with horror and fear of the savage who leered down at him.

Save for the brisk crackle of the flames the night seemed charged with an awful stillness. The moon was fleeced with clouds, and a faint rising breeze soughed insistently through the bush and the crested lantanas.

From windward the deep ocean swell surged in, breaking against the lower cliffs with slow, thunderous resonance. The *John Foster* had become quiet.

"Speak up!" snarled the skipper, giving Blake another kick. "Where's that loot stowed?"

"I don't know," and Blake writhed under the pain. "But I'd give a good deal for five minutes bare-handed with you!"

Marshall glared, his eyes bloodshot and red in the fire-glow, half-hidden brutality flashing out in every line of his powerful, wolfish features. Then he turned to his men, who were crowding in with brutish eagerness for the spectacle.

"Two o' you men lay out along the beach, with rifles — one each way. Sharp, you swine! Keep watch, or I'll flake ye! Where's that cursed Paddy Ryan? Any o' you lads do for him?"

"We met him up in the bush, sir," spoke up one of Bower's men. "Said he was —"

"Yes," raved Steelfist, "an' then he let out a yell for Dude, huh? No, you didn't know better'n to let him pass, drat ye! An' the bo'sun — anybody seen him?"

Nobody had, it appeared.

Blake looked at the girl, met her eyes, and groaned to himself. He was helpless, unable to move, and the look in her eyes, the dread pallor of her features, the brave hopelessness with which she held herself erect and unflinching — all these told him that she knew nothing of the gold, yet knew that Steelfist would never believe that she knew nothing of it.

"She's a brave heart — a brave heart!" thought Blake, watching her, fascinated. "Marshall knows it, too, and he'll think her lying — oh, the devil, the cursed devil! If I could get rid of these lashings for half a minute!"

But he could not.

With his sentries posted, and secure, as he thought, from all possible attack, Steelfist turned his attention to his prisoners.

The beach was flung into brilliant radiance by the licking tongues of fire; the brutal ferocity of the skipper was reflected in the faces around him. The scum of the two ships had clung to Marshall, and brandy and gold-lust had turned them into beasts.

"Now, my suckin' doves," and Steelfist leered wolfishly, "where's the gold that ought to been in that chest, huh? Speak up, Dude, or taste fire!"

"Go look for it, you dog!" snapped Blake, knowing that protests of ignorance were of no avail.

Marshall swung toward the girl.

"You, Mary Peabody! Want to see your fine friend toasted, huh? Then talk out an' do it lively! Where's the loot?"

"I do not know," said the girl quietly, holding herself very erect and firm.

"All right, curse you! Here — two o' you bullies shove the Dude into the embers over there — no, leave his boots on."

Two of the men seized Blake and thrust him forward, then tripped him up and shot him along the ground, feet first, into the heat of the fire. He heard a choking cry from Mary, as the embers and half-burned tangle covered his feet and ankles.

"Take him out — for God's sake don't do this! I'll give you the money — anything you want —"

"Out with him, bullies!" roared the skipper.

With the heat drawing a stifled groan of agony from him, Blake was dragged away from the fire; the men set up a yell at this evidence of the skipper's seeming success.

"Spit it out!" bellowed Marshall to the girl. "Where's the stuff? Out with it, or back he goes an' you with him!"

White-faced, stark with horror, she stared at him.

"I don't know where it is now," she broke out, "but I'll promise that Mr. Wicliff shall turn it over to you — you shall have the whole thing —"

"More o' your blasted lies!" screamed Marshall, his face that of a madman. "I'll learn ye to lie to me! In with 'em, bullies — move, curse you!"

Even the men hesitated at this order, but under a flood of oaths from Marshall they seized Mary Peabody and thrust her forward. Now Blake loosened his lips, and poured out his rage on Marshall, his words biting deep until the skipper's face swept with new passion.

"In with 'em!" he bellowed furiously. "Let 'em warm their feet at the same fire an' we'll get truth out of 'em —"

"The girl's gone, sir," spoke up a man, and the others hesitated.

Mary had fainted.

Marshall raised the rifle which he still held.

"Now," he yelled, "obey, you rats! Shove 'em in feet first, both together — an' do it lively!"

Blake felt himself gripped, and raved out incoherent curses. He saw Slim Jack lifting his feet for the fling, and — something long and thin seemed to flicker through the air.

Slim Jack dropped his feet suddenly and looked surprised, caught at the end of a shark-tooth spear that had gone clear through him, and fell forward into the fire.

CHAPTER XVII
TO A FINISH

Before any of the watching group quite realized what had happened, a heavy coco-wood club flew from the edge of the jungle, struck Marshall, and sent him sprawling on the sand, his rifle flying away.

After the club came Fancy Harry Lovell, a stream of brown figures followed the bo'sun with a wild yell, revolvers cracked, and the fight was on.

In that first moment of torture Blake's ankle-lashings had been burned through. Now he tried to gain his feet, but fell back with a groan of agony; his burns effectually kept him out of the turmoil.

Some one gripped his shoulder, he felt himself dragged roughly over the sand; then appeared Wicliff, who had rescued Mary Peabody from the trampling horde. Holding the unconscious girl in his arms, he joined Blake, who lay watching.

No word was spoken; indeed, Blake gave the old missionary but a glance, for he was intent on the fight and was lending the encouragement of his voice to his own men — Ryan and Ole Kafban being with Lovell.

In that first moment, Marshall's men were all but overcome by the sheer surprise of the assault, and Ryan shot two of them mercilessly.

Then the skipper was up, and the terrible steel fist came into play. Ryan was knocked senseless. Ole came staggering blindly toward Blake, and dropped to the sand groaning, a ragged cut from temple to chin.

"Into 'em, bullies!" roared Steelfist, setting the example.

Though it was long since Wicliff's natives had wielded spear and club, they evinced a lust for battle that staggered the seamen. There was no chance for rifles, save as clubs; the natives had surrounded the party from the ships, cutting them off from the boats; and, though but a dozen in all, followed the lead of Fancy Harry nobly.

Desperate, the seamen whipped out knife and clubbed rifle, and fought for their lives. Lovell, revolver in hand, went down under the rush. A stalwart native smashed down a seaman with a huge club and drove in at Steelfist; the skipper leaped nimbly aside, whirled, and sent his terrible right from the shoulder.

As the native crumpled up and fell in a heap, a wild snarl of triumph broke from Marshall.

"Into 'em, lads — knife the cursed rats!"

Blake turned his head, desperation in his eyes, and sought the *John Foster*. He prayed that young Boston would come — but the lagoon was silent, empty of boats. Boston and his men were either drunk or heedless of the fracas.

There came a crack and a rifle-flame thirty feet away; the two sentries sent out by Marshall were coming in. So suddenly had the whole thing passed, that only now had they realized what was up.

Blake writhed up against the missionary.

"For God's sake, loose my hands!" he cried. "There's Ryan over there, knocked out — he must have a revolver about him, for I gave him one! Hurry up — loose me and give me a gun, Wicliff!"

Something like a groan broke from the gaunt missionary, but his trembling fingers worked at Blake's wrists.

"I have no strength," he muttered in Blake's ear. "I've been tramping with my boys all night, making sure all was safe — then we found Mary gone, and there was more searching — your man Ryan found us just in time —"

"Get me that gun!" cried Blake, as his hands came free.

Setting down the form of the girl, Wicliff obeyed. Even in the firelight Blake could see that the man had aged terribly since their last meeting, and must be very weak.

Searching Ryan, who had been flung out of the fight, senseless, Wicliff found the revolver, and came back. Meantime, Marshall had been working havoc among the natives, his blood-streaked face like that of a demon; Lovell encountered him, stood up to him for a moment and slugged toe to toe — only to go down beneath a clubbed rifle from behind.

Blake lifted his revolver, coolly, his hand steady. He threw down on the rifleman running from the south end of the beach, and the man dropped to the shot. Turning, he picked off the man who had clubbed Lovell and sought to get a shot at Steelfist.

But the skipper had heard those reports and had learned their cause. He came around with a roar, turned his back on the fight and leaped at Blake, cursing as he came.

Lips compressed, eyes narrowed, Blake waited — he must be sure of his shot this time. When the raging Marshall was two yards away, he pulled trigger. The hammer clicked emptily — the last cartridge was gone!

Before Blake could move that steel fist had crashed into his cheek and knocked him sprawling on the sand.

He got to his knees, desperate with the agony of his burned feet, to see Marshall turn on the motionless Wicliff. Wild with pain and rage, Blake tottered up and fell on the skipper with one terrible blow flush to the jaw.

Steelfist reeled, came back, and Blake, unable to guard, caught a short-arm jab that hurled him down again. He was done and knew it; sobbing with his very impotency, he dragged himself up to his elbow. But Marshall gave him no further thought.

"Now, you cursed gospel-shark," bellowed the maddened skipper, "it's lights out for you an' this —"

And then came Ole.

Bleeding horribly from his jagged face-long wound, the Finn, who must have come to himself a moment before, rose from the sand. His peaked face and watery eyes gleamed with berserk madness, he mouthed inarticulate yells that were more horrible than words, and his sheath knife glowed in the firelight.

Marshall heard those yells and turned barely in time. Ole came in with a leap and a swift upward stab that had meant death to an ordinary man. But Steelfist, snarling, caught the thrust in the steel and leather harness of his right hand and wrenched the knife free. It fell at Wicliff's feet.

Swift as a flash Marshall stooped, caught up the weapon and slashed down at the white figure of the girl. The stroke went home — in the shoulder of the Finn, who had flung himself desperately in between.

"Ay pay ju oudt!" he screamed, rising.

"Look out!" yelled Blake in warning.

The maddened men were past all warning, however. There was a sickening thud as Marshall's steel fist drove home with awful force and crushed in the breastbone of the Finn.

Sorely stricken, Ole staggered back, but his hand was tugging at the knife fastened in his flesh, and he tore it free. Then, with a sobbing cry of desperation, he flung himself bodily at the skipper.

Blake was dimly aware that Steelfist's mad fury had drawn all eyes toward him, that the fight was hanging fire; but he, with all the rest, was watching tensely the two men who gripped each other to the death.

Ole had fastened to Marshall's throat, careless of blows; his left hand was sunk like a claw into the powerful neck of his erstwhile torturer, and he was growling like some maddened animal.

"Blast ye — git away —"

The labored breath of the skipper whistled from his great chest as he fought to batter his clinging enemy loose; more than ever did Steelfist Marshall resemble a wolf in that moment, as he drew himself up and back, striving to get free of those gripping, death-clenched fingers.

Again and again his terrible steel hand crunched into Ole's broken body. The Finn's growl turned to a whining groan with the agony of his shattered breast — racking sobs burst from him.

Yet he held on; all his vitality seemed concentrated into one intense spark, destined to bore through Marshall's strength as a carbon point bores through chilled steel.

The horrible, wordless struggle had swift ending. The Finn's right hand came free of Marshall's clutch, and the knife flashed to the skipper's bent-back head. Death laid hold on Ole Kafban, and he fell under the last blow of the steel fist — fell like a limp thing, lying in a heap on the sand.

For an instant Steelfist Marshall stood upright, plucking at his throat. A cry of horror broke from some one, and Blake echoed it. From the skipper's mouth protruded Ole's knife-haft — the blade had gone true, through mouth to brain. With never a word more, Marshall went to his knees, and then fell forward on his face, dead.

For one tense moment the watching men stood paralyzed, awed. A great scream rang out, and Marshall's men went to pieces; they fled into the bush, up and down the beach, shrieking over that they had seen.

Blake dragged himself forward. From the water came a sudden sound of oars and a hoarse hail.

"Dude — hey, Dude! It's me, young Boston! Want us?"

But Blake did not answer. All things were dim to him, of a sudden; he heard Wicliff calling to the natives and then found that which he had sought.

He lay motionless, pressing the hand of Mary Peabody to his brow, thanking God that she had not witnessed that last horror.

CHAPTER XVIII

ONCE MORE AFLOAT

"I think that the only brave man in all this mess has been Ole Kafban," said Blake, gazing at the shore.

"So?" Mary Peabody took his hand in hers, smiling a little as she drew his eyes to her face. "No, Jack dear — I think you're the bravest of all."

Blake looked at her in some surprise. In the three weeks which had elapsed since that terrible and memorable night, the girl had ever been the first to give to Ole Kafban his meed of tribute.

"Eh, Mary?" His gray eyes were puzzled, "You know that isn't —"

"You foolish man!" and she laughed swiftly. "Weren't you brave enough to marry me this morning? Be careful! There's Mr. Wicliff's boat coming out — and all these men —"

Blake drew back, smiling.

"Sorry you married me, Mary?"

She studied him for a moment, her eyes twinkling.

"No — not yet, sir!"

She flashed down the ladder to the gangway, as Wicliff's boat approached. Blake turned, his eyes narrowing suddenly at a voice behind.

"Mr. Blake — beggin' your pardon, sir, does Mr. Wicliff sail with us?"

It was a new Bully Forrester whom Blake eyed.

One arm, broken when the *Marshall* was blown up, was still in a sling; while two weeks in irons had not only completely broken the spirit of the bucko mate, but had brought to him the lasting realization that the erstwhile Dude was now master of the ship. Hence, Forrester had capitulated without honors, and Blake was seeing that he kept in that condition.

"I think he's come out to say good-by, Forrester. Go ahead — heave up short and wait for the word."

The pitifully small crew sprang to the capstan, Fancy Harry Lowell taking second mate's position with a smirk of importance.

Jack shook hands with Wicliff, as the old missionary came forward.

"Glad to see you again, sir! Any word from those men that were with Marshall that last night? Are they still hiding out on the south headland?"

Wicliff nodded. "Yes, they're adrift down there still, but they're all right, Blake."

"Sure you don't want me to take them off for you?" smiled Blake. "I can land my men and rout 'em out in no time, in spite of their guns."

Wicliff's piercing blue eyes twinkled as he glanced from Blake to

Mary, who had that morning become Mrs. Blake.

"No, I have use for them, and wish no more conflict."

"Come, man!" laughed Blake, puzzled. "What on earth do you expect to use them at? They'll resist arrest and raid your fields —"

"Tut, tut, sir!" broke in Wicliff. "I am not too old yet to convert men, sir, and it seems those men are badly in need of it."

Blake's face went grave.

"You'll never do it, Wicliff, never in the world! They're waterfront sweepings, wharf-rats — why, no man on earth could put the fear of God into those scoundrels!"

The other nodded quietly.

"I quite agree with you there. No man could do it. But has it occurred to you that God might accomplish something of the sort Himself, in His own good time?"

Blake's eyes shifted to the rugged grandeur of the hinterland, glowing in the noonday sun. He nodded quietly.

"Well, I'll be off," and Wicliff took the girl in his arms, looked deep into her eyes, then pressed his lips to her brow. "God bless you, both! And remember, I can get letters twice a year!"

"We'll remember it, never fear," said Mary softly, as Wicliff shook hands with Blake and turned to the gangway. "Good-by! Good-by?"

"Anchor's apeak, sir!" snapped Lovell, from forward.

Blake signed to Forrester.

"Break her out, bullies! H'ist away tops'ls!"

The halyards were manned with a whoop, and Paddy Ryan started the chorus that jerked the main topsail aloft.

> "Oh, come all you little yaller boys,
> An' roll the cotton down!
> Oh, a husky pull, my bully boys,
> An' roll the cotton down!"

With her three topsails mastheaded and the fore-topsail laid to the mast, the cable was broken out, the fore-braces came in hand over hand, and the ship swung on her heel, leaning gracefully to the freshening breeze.

Blake stood at the poop rail, Mary's hand in his, and together they waved a last farewell to Wicliff's dancing boat. Bully Forrester approached and touched his cap.

"What port, sir?" he asked, grinning.

Blake looked into the girl's brown eyes.

"What port, captain?"

Their eyes met and held for a long moment. Then —

"Home, dear!"

THE END

www.ingramcontent.com/pod-product-compliance
Ingram Content Group UK Ltd.
Pitfield, Milton Keynes, MK11 3LW, UK
UKHW041435180426
11947UKWH00007B/461